the Poisoned House

by MICHAEL FORD

Library of Congress Cataloging-in-Publication Data

Ford, Michael, 1980-
The poisoned house / by Michael Ford.
p. cm.
Summary: As the widowed master of an elegant house in Victorian-era
London slips slowly into madness and his tyrannical housekeeper takes on
more power, a ghostly presence distracts a teenaged maidservant with clues
to a deadly secret.
ISBN 978-0-8075-6589-6 (hard cover)
[1. Household employees—Fiction. 2. Ghosts—Fiction.
3. Supernatural—Fiction. 4. London (England)—History—
19th century—Fiction. 5. Great Britain—History—Victoria, 1837-1901—
Fiction.] I. Title.
PZ7.F75328Po 2011
[Fic]—dc22
2010048250

For more information about Albert Whitman & Company,
visit our web site at www.albertwhitman.com.

To Mum and Dad

The following papers were kindly donated to the Municipal Library by Anne Merchant, the current owner of 112 Park Avenue, the property formerly known as Greave Hall. The papers were reportedly uncovered during renovation of the house, in the locked drawer of a bureau in the attic. They appear to record several months in the year 1855 of the life of a teenage girl called Abigail Tamper, who lived and worked at that address. Every effort has been made to transcribe faithfully the details of the handwritten manuscript.

Many people and events within the script are difficult to verify with certainty, although investigations are ongoing. Pages from the original can be viewed in situ at the discretion of the librarian.

Emily Verbeck
Assistant Curator
Victorian manuscripts

One

THE STONE STEPS TO THE BASEMENT WERE ICE-cold under my bare feet. In the scullery, the copper gleamed dimly and the floor hadn't been swept. Through the kitchen wall, Cook was snoring. If she'd taken her normal measure of gin before falling into bed, then she'd sleep through a hurricane.

Rowena brushed past my leg, purring softly, so I bent down and stroked her beneath the chin. I'd named her myself when she was found skulking around the stables three years before. She was fat now, and I was sorry I wouldn't get to know her little kittens when they came.

I unbolted the coal store door and pushed it open inch by inch. A cold draft of coal dust blew over me, the smell reminding me of Adam, the delivery boy. The stores were low, so it wasn't hard to clamber over the top and push open the hatch. I climbed out under a starlit sky.

I let the hatch close as slowly as if it were made of porcelain, then headed across the yard to the main gate. The hinges gave a tiny squeak and then I was out on the road. I crossed it and slid down the bank into the Park.

The sack on my back already felt heavy. In it were my best dress and the cardigan knitted by my mother, together with my father's watch, half a loaf of stale bread and a jar of pickles. I had no money—Mrs. Cotton kept all my wages, and it would have made her suspicious had I asked for them.

I'd promised myself I wouldn't look back, but halfway across the Park, in the shadow of a plane tree, I couldn't help myself. The lake was still as a mirror, and through the hushed pools of light from the gas lamps on the far side of the road, Greave Hall loomed dormant in darkness, the windows black.

No, not all of them.

A yellow glow spread behind the curtain upstairs. Her bedroom.

For several seconds, my feet seemed as rooted as the tree I rested by. I watched the faint glimmer of a candle. How could she have known?

"Abi!" called a man's voice. "Abigail?"

It was Rob Willmett, the footman. Mrs. Cotton had him up already.

I turned and ran, my pumps slapping on the path.

The gates on to the road were locked, but I didn't have much flesh on my bones. I pushed a leg between the cold cast-iron railings and squeezed through.

On the other side, I sprinted across the deserted Mall. To my right, Horse Guards Parade was empty and silent. It had been eleven months since we were permitted half a day to watch the soldiers at their exercises. His Lordship's son, Samuel, had been among them. I'd write to him, I thought, just to let him know I was all right. That is, if he ever came back at all.

A police whistle trilled far off. Surely not looking for me? Not already?

The struts and beams of the new station at Charing Cross rose in the darkness behind. I ran across a square. It was New Year's Day in the year of Our Lord 1855 and on the ground lay remnants of the previous night's celebration: shreds of bunting, bones of fish and fowl and rotting fruit aplenty. I picked my way through them and reached the pedestal where the statue of Charles I sits in his saddle. Rob used to say they erected the statue without a head, as a reminder of the king's death. He was joking with me, like he always did.

I heard the clip-clop of iron-shod hooves and another whistle, closer this time. I flattened myself against the statue's base, and watched my breath curl off into the night. There was nowhere to go without being seen.

"Miss Tamper!" called a deep voice—not Rob's. "Miss Tamper! Are you here?"

I took small steps along my hiding place, tracing the stone with my fingertips, until I could look out from behind the statue's base. Coming off the Mall, and carrying a lantern in one hand, was a constable on his mount. His tone was stern. "You don't want to cause trouble for His Lordship, Miss Tamper."

I ducked back out of sight.

Not for Lord Greave, no. But if Mrs. Cotton lost any sleep, then I wouldn't let my conscience dwell on it.

"Come home now, Abigail, and all will be well." His words were breathless and impatient.

A half-rotten turnip lay on the ground by my foot. I crouched and picked it up. Assaulting a member of Her Majesty's finest was not in my upbringing, but at that moment Greave Hall held a good deal more dread for me than the law.

I peeked again at the mounted officer. The horse twitched its head towards me and snorted through wide nostrils.The man turned as well.

"There you are, young lady," he said. "That's enough nonsense for tonight, no?"

"I won't go back," I whispered, steeling myself as much as addressing the constable.

"What's that, miss?" He spurred his horse in my direction and set it at a shambling gait. With each step the lantern in his hand rocked back and forth.

"I won't go back!" I shouted. I hurled the vegetable right at him. My aim was good, and it smacked into his shoulder, knocking the lantern from his hand. The glass smashed on the stone, sucking the light away.

"What's this?" he cried.

His horse reared, wheeling from the ground, and the constable lost his saddle, landing with a great thump in the road.

Any sympathy I had for him flared and died like a candle caught in a draft, and I was off between two bollard posts quicker than a hare.

"Wait there!" he bellowed. "Assault!"

The alley was dark, and the doors on either side were bolted shut. The smell of animals—wet fur and feed—was thick in the air, and the ground pockmarked with puddles. I ran through them, the filthy water splashing my stockings and surely ruining my shoes.

I heard the policeman's heavy feet behind.

The alley branched two ways and I took the passage on the left. It was narrower still, and a trail of squeaking rats scurried out of my path. I lost track of the turns I followed, and didn't stop to check my progress until I reached the backyard of a tavern called The Fiddler. I jumped a barrow left outside and skidded up against a rough door. I found a sodden, split barrel and crouched behind it, ears afire for any sound.

I stayed there while the sweat cooled on my forehead. After a few minutes I was sure the policeman wasn't following, so I got up and walked off, finding a wider, but unlit street of houses. My clothes were ragged and my body ached from toe to crown. I was completely lost but I felt no fear. I was farther from Greave Hall than ever before.

When morning came, I told myself, I'd look for somewhere to change my soiled clothes, then begin the search for a new place.

My name would have to change, of course, and without references I could hope for little better than parlor maid duties. But I was fifteen in six weeks, and in time I could hope for advancement.

A hand fell on my shoulder.

"Hello, Miss Tamper."

I squealed and spun round. The constable's hat was askew and his face flushed dark with anger. I pulled away, but his grip was strong.

"Let me go!" I cried.

"I'm taking you home to Greave Hall, Miss Tamper," he said, dragging me by my arm.

I fought him, kicking at his legs and thumping against his chest. I'm ashamed to say I became like an animal, and even tried to sink my teeth into his arm.

"It's not my home!" I screamed. "I won't go back!"

Two

I MUST HAVE FALLEN INTO A FAINT. The sharp stink of hartshorn woke me, and I opened my eyes to the face of a man I recognised, but whose name I couldn't recall. About fifty years of age, with a grave expression, he wore a tie under his thick white beard. Though indoors, he hadn't removed his hat.

". . . and this mark, Mrs. Cotton," he was saying. "How did she get this?"

The man's cool fingers pressed lightly on my cheek. I winced. Mrs. Cotton had slapped me on Christmas Day, for slipping Rowena a scrap of beef. The bruise had spread across my cheek deep purple like a swollen storm cloud. In the days after it had faded to a sickly green tidemark.

"The child must have been running around the corridors after dark," replied Mrs. Cotton. "You've seen tonight how uncontrolled she is, Doctor."

It was Dr. Ingle, of course—His Lordship's physician. Was he here just for me?

I wanted to speak out, to tell him that the house-keeper was lying, but the words left my lips half asleep. I was lying on Cook's cot in the kitchen, and there was a blanket pulled up to my chin. The small wood fire was lit and crackling. Rob stood at one side, a head taller than Mrs. Cotton, whose eyes were like chips of coal, black and ready to burn.

"Well, I'm done here, Mrs. Cotton," said the doctor. "I think the young miss should be excused duties for the remainder of the day. There's nothing wrong with her as such, but her skin is pale and she's thin for her age." He looked at me over the top of his glasses for a moment. "Does she eat enough?"

"Her appetite is as healthy as Mr. Willmett's here," said Mrs. Cotton with a brittle laugh. I noticed now that she was wearing a thick housecoat over her nightgown. Her sister, His Lordship's wife Eleanor, had died many years before, and Mrs. Cotton liked to make use of the dead woman's wardrobe.

The doctor snapped his satchel shut and Rob stepped forward.

"Your payment, Dr. Ingle . . ."

His words met a raised hand. "See that Miss Tamper has a glass of warmed milk and some rest. Understood?"

Rob nodded.

I listened as their footsteps echoed in the servants' hall, and then up the main stairs. Mrs. Cotton's eyes settled on mine with a look I knew all too well. But I wasn't going to cry.

I heard the clatter of a pan behind me and raised myself on my elbow to see Cook bustling by the stove.

"Leave us, Deirdre," said Mrs. Cotton.

Cook paused, her back to me, "But Dr. Ingle said—"

"Leave us now, please," said Mrs. Cotton. The light from a candle played over the housekeeper's face as the tendons shifted under her skin.

Cook hung up the pan again and wrung her hands. She gave a quiet "Yes, ma'am," and was gone.

Mrs. Cotton slid in two short steps to my side, and took a seat on the bench, her back straight as a board. I pulled the blanket tighter around me.

"Where did you think you'd go, Miss Tamper?" she asked. Her voice was low, the anger restrained like water gathering at a dam, ready to burst.

"I just wanted some fresh air," I said. We both knew it wasn't true, but a lie seemed the only way. Her eyes blinked, and I saw the first flecks of fire in the black of her pupils.

"Some air." It was not a question, and her mouth twisted around the rotten taste of the words. "You are aware of the rules of this house, are you not?"

I nodded. I knew all the rules: no talking in the family rooms, no using the main stairs, no visitors, no speaking unless first spoken to, a smart appearance at all times. The list was never-ending.

But the rule she was referring to at that moment was no doubt the curfew. For me, it extended from eleven at night until six in the morning and was unbreakable.

Between those times, Greave Hall was my prison.

"You know," she said, almost wistfully, taking in the kitchen with a sweep of her eyes, "I don't think I even heard you. I just *knew* you were up to something. That's what makes me good at my job, Miss Tamper. I know everything that happens under this roof." Her eyes flicked on to me once more. "Did you really think I would just let you go?" I could tell she didn't want an answer, so I didn't speak. "How did you get out?" she asked.

She obviously hadn't seen the open bolt on the coal store. Well, I wasn't going to give her any satisfaction. I kept my silence, and her face hardened.

"It doesn't matter," she said.

Mrs. Cotton reached under her apron. I wandered if it was going to be the strip of leather, her favorite thrashing tool. Cold dread crept over my skin.

But it was worse. She pulled out a single folded sheet. I knew what it was immediately—the letter I'd tucked under Lizzy's door, ready for when she returned from New Year's at her sister's in Battersea.

The housekeeper reached to bring the lamp closer and opened the paper. She recited the letter in her cracked voice, measuring each word against the silence.

"'Dear Elizabeth, forgive me,'" she read. "'I cannot stay here any longer. By the time you read this, I will be gone. I hardly have to tell you why.'" Mrs. Cotton paused. She licked her lips. "'I doubt that they will try very hard to look for me—a scullery maid can be got in a matter of hours in London.

"'Until a replacement is found, I hope that you are not overburdened with my duties. Your loving friend, Abigail.'"

I swallowed and my throat tightened. I couldn't look into Mrs. Cotton's eyes any longer and instead stared at the paper clutched in her fingers, the signed admission of my guilt. If there had been more time, I would have chosen my words more carefully, but I'd wanted to get as far as possible before dawn.

"'P.S. Please burn this,'" she ended. "How clever of you."

My lip shook, but still I didn't cry. She held the letter above the candle flame. A corner blackened, then the fire took hold. As my words were consumed, she leaned over me and dropped the paper in the grate. "Your wish is fulfilled," she said.

The smoke from the charred paper was bitter.

Mrs. Cotton's hand smoothed my blanket and her eyes travelled from me to the doorway beyond, then back again. Her head cocked a fraction.

"And what did you say to Constable Armstrong, Abigail?"

Her voice was a whisper now, so that neither Cook nor Rob could overhear. I knew she was worried that I had given something away—about how she treated us, or how she abused her position in the house.

"I said nothing," I lied. The housekeeper didn't need to know about my helpless tears in front of the policeman, how I'd cursed her name and everything about my life at Greave Hall.

Her fingers found my arm beneath the blanket. I gasped as her nails dug into my skin. It felt as though she was trying to rip my flesh away.

Her expression was still as a portrait—only her eyes blazed.

"Nothing at all?" she asked.

"Not a thing!" I said, wriggling to free myself. The pain was like a burn from the stove, but it didn't stop. "Not a thing—I swear."

Mrs. Cotton released me and stood, turning away. She spoke to the whole room. "The constable was kind enough to forget this evening's unhappy incident," she said, "if only out of fondness for my brother."

Blood seeped from the half-moon gouges in my arm.

Brother-in-law, I thought. His Lordship is only stuck with you because his wife died.

"But I cannot be so lenient," continued Mrs. Cotton. "You have betrayed my trust, that of His Lordship and that of God." In that order, I supposed. "I have hardly had time to think about your punishment." Her eyes fell to something on the floor, and I pushed myself up to look. It was the hessian sack.

"Oh," she said. "I almost forgot."

She peered into the sack and shook her head. "What a pity," she said. "Your clothes are all crumpled!"

"I'll press them," I said.

She pulled out the cardigan. "And your mother made you this, didn't she?" There was a smile creeping around her lips.

"Yes, ma'am," I said.

She stood up, went to the little wood fire, and dropped it into the flames.

"No!" I said, jumping up.

The wool sizzled as it caught.

"I shall expect you to set the fires at half past five," said Mrs. Cotton."Now get yourself to bed."

She fixed me with a hawk-eyed glare as I made my way on unsteady feet to the scullery. I tried not to look at the fire and the cardigan that had smelled of my mother and now smelled of burnt straw. The bolt to the coal store, I saw, was pushed in. Someone was looking out for me, at least.

I took to the servants' stairs again, up to my room in the attic. Mrs. Cotton had thrown off the top sheet on my bed to reveal the rolled-up tablecloth beneath. I'd hoped it would look enough like a sleeping body to fool anyone checking.

Hot tears gathered behind my eyes, but I held them back. God knows I'd cried enough in the past year. No time for crying tonight.

I poured water from the jug and bathed my arm until the bleeding stopped. If she hated me so much, why couldn't she just let me go? Reliable staff were hard to come by, for sure, but finding someone to do the most menial jobs in the house wouldn't have taken long. The only conclusion I could reach was that she needed to be cruel to someone, and I filled that role so well.

I wound my father's watch. Ten turns as always, in remembrance of the man I'd never met. If he'd lived, perhaps things would have been different. My mother wouldn't have had to come and work at Greave Hall. She wouldn't have fallen ill. I'd likely never have met Mrs. Cotton.

Beneath me, the house went back to sleep as the clock chimed a distant three o'clock. In two and half hours, a new day would begin. It would be like every other—without hope, without respite. Without my mother.

The bed was damp as wet earth as I slipped between the sheets.

Three

I DREAMT THE SAME DREAM AS BEFORE.

My mother wakes me, calling me down in her lilting voice: "Snowdrop, where are you?" She calls me that because I was born in February, when the snowdrops flower in the Park.

It's cold in the room, and I climb from the bed stiffly. I check my father's watch and see that it's nearly six o'clock already! I pull on my work dress and hurry from the room. The stairs are steeper than usual, so steep that I have to turn around and climb down with my hands on each step, like a rock face.

"Come to me, little Snowdrop," calls my mother.

There are tears in my eyes—happy tears. She's downstairs. Not gone at all. There's been a mistake. She's alive!

I reach the landing, and there are the others: Lizzy,

Mr. Lock, Rob, even Cook. I don't stop to wonder why they're all up so early, or why they're all smiling.

"Go on, then," says Lizzy, nodding. "She's in the hall, waiting."

I round the top of the main staircase and look down. In my dream, it doesn't matter that these stairs aren't for servants. In dreams anything is possible, even the dead coming back to life.

The front door is open, and there she is. Mama. She's wearing a navy bonnet and a dress trimmed with lace. In her hand is a pastel blue parasol. She places it to one side and holds out her arms, beaming. "Hello, Snowdrop!"

With a surge of wind at my back, my feet leave the ground. I drift down the stairs, an inch above the steps.

My mother remains outside, still smiling. But as I come closer, the door begins to close. I try to lower my feet to the ground, to run, but I can only brush the carpet with my toes. I land just as the door shuts tight.

I reach for the handle, but it's not where it should be. The door has no handle at all. I claw at the crack in the frame, shouting, "Mama, I'm here! Don't go!"

Then the hairs on my neck prickle. I want to wake up, but I can't. And just as I realize there's no one on the other side of the door, I'm aware that someone else is standing behind me. I turn around.

I woke with my pulse thudding across my chest. Slowly, my eyes adjusted. The leaded frames of the tiny casement window looked like the bars of a prison, and the room seemed smaller than ever. It had once been set aside for sewing and my first memory, aged three or four, was sitting on that window ledge, gazing out over the trees while my mother sat in her rocking chair and sang to me.

My throat was parched. The sun wouldn't be up for quite some time, and I dressed shivering. I didn't need to check my watch—I woke at the same time every day without fail.

The scullery was freezing too, as if ice were about to form in the air. I pumped water through into the copper and lit the fire beneath it with a match from the box I kept in my apron.

Then I went from room to room on the ground floor, laying the fires. Mrs. Cotton suffered from poor circulation and liked all the fires lit, especially during the winter months. It was a boring daily routine—sifting the cinders, sweeping the ashes, refilling the scuttles and stoking, but these hours of darkness, before anyone else awoke, were my favorite. I could almost imagine that Greave Hall, with its grand rooms and tall ceilings, was my own.

The house awoke slowly around me. Cook was first, grunting a greeting as she splashed water over her face and rubbed the back of her neck. She was a great mountain of an Irishwoman, with a red complexion and untidy grey hair. She carried the scuttle through into the kitchen to light her own fire in the range. Then there were sounds from across the servants' hall. Mr. Lock walked in stiffly, dressed in his crumpled butler's outfit. I remember my mother saying he was once quite smart, handsome even, but he was in his sixties now and looked ten years older.

The minutes wore on, and a sense of familiar dread built in my stomach. Mrs. Cotton would be down soon. There was a housekeeper's room behind the butler's, but because she was as much family as staff, she'd taken a room on the first floor. Along with her dead sister's clothes, she claimed it as a right and Lord Greave, it seemed, had made no objection. "He wouldn't know if a troop of monkeys set up under his roof," Rob had said.

As I was lighting the sitting room fire, Rob, the footman emerged, half-dressed and carrying his bedroll, from the china closet where he slept. He had to stoop under the door frame and stopped to button up his shirt.

"How are you feeling this morning, m'lady?" he asked, grinning to show the gap between his two front teeth. He had always called me that, though Mrs. Cotton didn't like it.

"I'm well, thank you, Robert," I replied.

He paused and softened his smile, standing uncomfortably as though he expected me to say more— something about the events of the night before. I didn't.

"Right then," he said. "I shall give Lancelot his breakfast and see you in time."

"Oh, Rob," I said, "thank you for your help. With the bolt, I mean."

His brow creased. "The bolt?"

"To the coal store," I said. I explained that the housekeeper had wanted to know how I got out.

"Not me," he said. "Must have been Cook."

I returned to the fires, puzzled. Cook had never shown much warmth towards me, and I couldn't understand why she'd help in such a way.

The next fire to light was His Lordship's. I was about to leave the sitting room when I heard footsteps on the main stairs. They say birdwatchers can pick out the calls of birds in a forest. Well, after so long in a house you get to know who's coming by the sound of their feet, and this precise soft rhythm belonged to Mrs. Cotton. I stopped behind the door and waited for her to pass, as she always did, through the front hall and into the dining room. There she'd wait until the butler, Lock, brought her breakfast.

I hurried through the hallway and down to the basement, where I filled a jug with hot water for His Lordship's morning wash. Mr. Lock was too infirm to carry it up the stairs any more, and after several unfortunate spillages the role had gradually fallen to me on three days of the week and Rob on the others. I took the steps carefully—I didn't want to give Mrs. Cotton any more excuses for reprimanding me.

Lord Greave should, as master of the house, have taken a grander bedroom on the floor below, but with the death of his wife Eleanor almost twenty years before, he'd asked for a room to be renovated in the attic space, on the opposite side of the house from Lizzy and me. It was small, nestled up in the eaves, and was kept snug by a fireplace.

Upstairs, I laid the bowl down outside His Lordship's door and gave three knocks.

"Enter," said a cracked voice.

It was dark inside, the thick curtains drawn over the

single window, the air heavy and warm. Lord Greave lay in the center of his bed, his two pillows propping up a pale face just visible like the moon in an overcast sky.

"Good day Susan," he said.

"It's Abigail, Your Lordship," I said, setting down the jug beside his washstand. "Susan was my mother. She's passed on, sir. More than a year ago."

He rolled his head across the pillow on the stiff hinges of his neck. I couldn't see his eyes, but I could feel them on me.

"So she did, Abigail," he said. "So she did."

Without waiting for further instruction, I made my way to the fireplace. Either Lock or Rob had laid the fire the previous evening, so it was a quick job to get it started. I went to the curtains next and drew one aside. A shaft of pale morning light fell across the floor.

"No!" Lord Greave cried out.

He thrashed under his sheets, wailing as though bathed in fire. "No! No light! Close it, damn you!"

I pulled the drape, and the room was dark again. I could see his shadowy figure sitting up in bed, like some petrified shrunken goblin. His top half was unclothed and I turned away, ashamed. It wasn't right for a servant to see her master in such a condition.

"Will there be anything else, sir?" I asked.

He didn't answer, though I could hear his slow breathing.

"Very good, sir." I tiptoed out of the room, glad to close the door behind me.

Four

WHEN I REACHED THE SCULLERY AGAIN ROB WAS
back inside, his cheeks flushed. Rowena was winding
around his feet, her belly hanging low.

"By God it's cold out there," said Rob. "How's the
master?"

"Bad," I said. "He didn't want any light in the room."

Cook and Rob shared a look. "He suffering for the
boy," said Deirdre. "Fading away. If Samuel don't come
back safe it'll be the end of His Lordship, mark my words."

Two loaves of bread were cooling on the side. I hadn't
eaten since nine the previous night, and with three hours
of work behind me, my stomach was a hard knot. It made
a sound like distant thunder.

"Go on then, will you," said Cook. "Mrs. Cotton's
eating hers and you may not get a chance later. There's
dripping in the pantry."

I found the dish on the shelves and perched on the bench beside Rob. He cut the bread and I smeared over a layer of the goose fat left from Christmas. We didn't get much time for meals—it was a case of fitting them in around chores. Mrs. Cotton didn't like to see us eat.

I was finishing my second slice when there was a knock at the downstairs door.

"That'll be the coalman," said Rob. "Tell him we only need a couple of sackfuls to keep us to Monday. And mind he doesn't wipe his hand on the door frame."

Adam was waiting outside, hopping from foot to foot, with his hands in his armpits. His face was almost black for coal dust, which made his eyes seem to glow white. Despite his grubby appearance, he was a ray of sunshine in my life and a reminder that there were others worse off than myself. Both Adam's parents were dead too, and he'd been plucked from the workhouse by a coal higgler and grocer with the unfortunate name of Crook, to help on his errands. Behind him in the lane was the coal cart and Archer the carthorse, head bowed into his nosebag.

"Morning, Adam," I said.

"Bloody freezing!" said Adam, looking past me longingly. "What's it like in the lap o'luxury, hey?"

"Well," I replied, putting on a posh voice, "the caviar

jelly we had last night was ruined by the presentation. You know I can't eat except off a gold-plated spoon."

We both laughed. "We'll need two hundredweight, please."

Adam returned to the cart and came back lugging the bags. He lifted the hatch, emptying them in. It seemed odd that only last night I'd crawled through the same way.

A cloud of coal dust rose up around him.

"Guess where I was yesterday?" he panted.

Adam claimed to be fourteen like me, but he was still half a head shorter. I took most things he said with a pinch of salt.

I put my hands on my hips and gave him the wryest expression I could muster.

"Buckingham Palace?" I said. "No, let me guess. The theater?"

"Chuckle, chuckle," he said. "Actually, Miss Tamper," he went on, leaning against the door frame until I pushed his black fingers away, "I went with the old Mr. Crook to—"

"Enough chatter," said Mrs. Cotton icily from the door.

That was Adam's signal to leave. He skipped out of the gate with a cheeky grin and I locked it after him. He was humming a song to himself as he led Archer by the reins. I envied his freedom to come and go as he pleased.

I went out to sweep and scrub the front step at nine. It didn't matter what happened behind closed doors, but to show a clean step to the world was supposed to mean something. Anyway, with the various postal deliveries or occasional visitors, the steps soon became scuffed.

"Happy New Year!" said a voice.

I looked up to see Lizzy standing there with a little case. Elizabeth had come to work in Greave Hall in around 1852. She was three years older than me, seventeen to my fourteen, and had been forced into service when her father was hurt in a factory accident. She had straight brown hair that she pinned up when working, almost black almond-shaped eyes and a kind face. She was a plump girl, with rosy cheeks and a soft way of talking. Her mother was lost long ago to the workhouse, but she had a sister living over the river, with a young baby and a wastrel husband. Though Lizzy never spoke about it, I knew that at least half her wages went to make up for what he drank away.

The sight of her smiling face made me feel ashamed. If things had worked out differently, she would be returning to a house in panic and a note saying goodbye.

"And a Happy New Year to you," I replied, then lowered my voice. "Mrs. Cotton's not at home, you'll be pleased to know."

Lizzy smiled and held up the case. "I've got a new hairbrush and two pairs of warm stockings. There's a comb for you too."

I stood up and left the scouring brush and cloth to give her a hug.

"Something happened," I said. "Last night."

"Oh?" Lizzy said, worry creasing her eyes and looking past me into the house. "Is everyone all right?"

"They're all fine," I said. "Rob will tell you, I'm sure."

I finished up the steps on my hands and knees. By the time I was done my fingers were red and aching. I swept the dust and leaves out into the road.

I saw Mrs. Cotton approaching from a distance, huddled into her new mink coat. I hurried inside.

The first post arrived at ten. His Lordship hardly sent any letters now, and in the past year the incoming correspondence had dropped too. Some days we received no post at all. That day there was just one letter, and Mr. Lock took it straight up to the attic. Shortly after he came to Mrs. Cotton's side and asked in a whisper if he could have a word with her in private. I wasn't eavesdropping, but there was a sense of urgency in his tone that made me turn from my boot polishing. Normally Mr. Lock did not speak to Mrs. Cotton unless absolutely necessary. I saw in his face a glimmer of excitement. Even the deep dark pouches beneath his eyes seemed to have lifted.

I looked across at Cook, but she was busy rolling pastry. If she had picked up on the flicker of electricity in the air, she concealed it well.

Rob was sent to harness Lancelot, grumbling about His Lordship's whims. When Mrs. Cotton came back below stairs, her movements were more brisk than usual. Lizzy was following in her wake. We were told to gather in the servants' hall, the open area at the bottom of the main stairs.

"I have important news," said Mrs. Cotton. "His Lordship has received a communication. From the War Office."

Samuel. It had to be. I felt suddenly afraid. Had poor Sammy been killed? Cook's hand covered her open mouth with a whimper; he was a favorite with her. The image of Samuel dressed in his uniform on his going-out parade flashed across my mind. God help us if something bad had happened.

"His Lordship's son is returning from the Crimea," said Mrs. Cotton, bringing a sigh of relief from us all, "but he's been wounded. How badly, we're not sure. Rob is taking His Lordship to the War Office to find out any more details they may have and it's up to all of us to make preparations for his return. Elizabeth, Abigail—I'll need you to make sure everything is ready."

"He will live though, will he not?" asked Cook.

She would not normally have dared interrupt Mrs. Cotton, but the housekeeper didn't even turn to look at her. She stared instead at me.

"We don't know yet," she said, "and it's not our place to speculate. His Lordship requires that you all go about your duties as usual until we have further news."

As she left up the main stairs, we traipsed into the kitchen. Cook sagged onto her bench.

"I pray to God he's all right," she said. "If he were to die—oh, it would be too much!"

"For His Lordship too, I reckon," said Rob grimly.

"It'd fair finish him off."

Mr. Lock grunted. "Let's not have such talk, Mr. Willmett."

"We don't know that he's very bad," said Lizzy, stroking Cook's shoulder. "Many men come back from fighting and make good lives for themselves. Samuel always was a strong lad, wasn't he?"

I was silent. Poor Sammy. I suppose I already thought he couldn't be too bad. They wouldn't bring him home if he was near death's door, would they? Despite my anxieties, the thought of having him home brought a smile to my lips. I was staff and he was master, but he was like a brother to me too—a friend whom I could trust. He'd been called up just about the time my mother fell ill, and afterwards I'd wished so much that he could have been there in those dark days. Now he was coming back, the balance of power in the house might shift again.

No wonder Mrs. Cotton didn't look happy.

Five

WE WERE TOLD TO HAVE A BEDROOM MADE UP
for Samuel's return, but not his former chamber.

"In the library, if you please," said Mrs. Cotton.

Lizzy and I shared a look. Did this mean he didn't
even have the strength to climb the stairs?

Men were brought in to help dismantle the bed and
bring the pieces down under Mr. Lock's supervision.
Attending to His Lordship's strange and infrequent
whims was hardly tiring, and for months the butler had
wandered aimlessly from room to room, searching for a
purpose to fill his day. Now he seemed to have it.

Lizzy and I carried down the clothes and bed linen
and made sure the room was comfortable. The library
was seldom used anyhow, and Mrs. Cotton demanded
we give it a thorough cleaning to make it habitable for a
convalescent. As a girl I had been allowed to take books

from the shelves on occasion, and as a consequence, while neither Rob nor Lizzy knew their letters, I could read and my handwriting was passable.

Not that I had much opportunity to put it to use.

The bed was placed opposite the bay window that looked out into the garden, far from any drafts which might slow Samuel's recovery. A tin bath was brought down from his room too, and scrubbed clean. At least we wouldn't have to carry the water up more than a single flight of stairs.

Over the course of the morning, running to and fro, Lizzy must have heard from Rob or Cook about the events of the night before, because as we were laying linen on the reassembled bed, she put a hand on my arm and kissed the top of my head.

"You could have come to me," she said. "We might have talked."

It was hard to meet her eyes, so full of generosity that I hardly deserved. "I'm sorry," I said. "I wasn't thinking straight."

"It sounds like you thought it through clearly enough," said Lizzy. "But what would you have done? Where would you have slept? It's the middle of winter, Abi!"

I knew she spoke only out of kindness, but her

words made me realize just how foolish I'd been. In all likelihood, I would have frozen to death by the morning.

"I—"

"Abigail," said Mrs. Cotton briskly, "carry the tea leaves and polishes upstairs—you can help me with the empty rooms today."

We both turned at once to see the housekeeper standing just inside the door, her bone-white hands clasped over her apron. I hadn't even heard her arrive, and wondered if she had overheard our talk. She moved like that sometimes, slipping silently between the rooms like a draft of malice.

"Yes, ma'am," I replied.

As I gathered the things we'd need from the scullery cupboard, Rob, who was painting varnish onto a chairleg, leaned close to me. "Watch out for anything . . . unusual, won't you?"

I gave him a puzzled look. "What do you mean?"

Rob shrugged and smiled. "Only that Mrs. Cotton might get a fright today."

A fright? I hurried up the stairs, where Mrs. Cotton waited outside the chamber formerly occupied by His Lordship's wife. I didn't remember her, of course, because she had died before I even came to Greave Hall, but her picture still hung on the stairs. My mother told me that she had never recovered from Samuel's birth, and was confined to her bed for some three months before dying.

We all knew that Mrs. Cotton didn't like going into the room alone. She'd been called in to attend on her sister through her illness and look after the baby Samuel, and had never left after Eleanor Greave's death. If it hadn't been for those sad circumstances, my mother, Susan Tamper, would never have come to Greave Hall herself. Sammy didn't take to his aunt, nor she to him, so when he was three it was decided that a day nurse was needed and my mother stepped into the role. Though it wasn't much, she and my father were glad of the extra money.

Mrs. Cotton slipped the key into the lock and pushed the door open, letting me pass through first. In the tilting mirror opposite, I saw her cross herself and mutter some silent words before following me in.

Certainly it was cold in there, almost like walking outdoors, and I could see my breath in the air. I used to think that death lingered in a place. Unlike the rest of the house we only cleaned this room, and the small adjoining nursery, once a week. The chamber had not been used since.

"Clean the nursery first," said Mrs. Cotton, scanning

the room quickly. "I'll be back shortly to check."

The nursery brought back painful memories for me, and Mrs. Cotton knew that. It was here that Samuel had spent his first years. Later, when he took a larger room at the front of the house, it became my room. My mother had died in the throes of cholera in the nurse's chamber next door.

It wasn't only that. The room also reminded me of the carefree childhood I had lost. My mother had told me the story many times, to make me know how lucky we were. When she told Lord Greave that she was pregnant, a few months after my father's death, she expected to be thrown out at once, for who would want a nurse with her own baby? But by then little Samuel had already taken a shine to her, and so it was decided that she could stay on permanently, moving into Greave Hall. Goodness knows how she coped! My mother never tired of describing Mrs. Cotton's face when she heard of the planned arrangement. Nothing could have been further from the housekeeper's sense of decorum. I could imagine her biting her tongue but wanting more than ever to counsel His Lordship about the proper etiquette. A servant's child, living under his roof? Indeed!

In some ways, Mrs. Cotton and I were the same.

We both lived on the fringes of the family and were afforded privileges unheard of for servants. Between the ages of one and ten I lived a blessed life. Mama and I never ate with the family, of course, but took our meals with the other servants, and when I was old enough I took a share of the chores. But Sammy looked after me, and His Lordship always gave me a fond smile. How Mrs. Cotton seethed!

Now, though, both of my protectors were gone.

I set about cleaning the nursery and nurse's room. Both were joined to Lady Greave's former bedroom, so the mistress of the house could see her child if she wished. Somehow, dust got in here too.

I spread damp tea leaves on the floor, then brushed them across the carpet to fetch up the dust. I was sweeping them back into the pan when I heard a wail from the room next door. Rushing in, I found Mrs. Cotton pressed against the wall with her hand to her throat. She glanced at me and pointed at the wardrobe —the door was open. "What is it?" I asked.

"You did this, Abigail Tamper!" she said.

"Pardon, ma'am?" I said. "Did what?"

She approached the wardrobe slowly and pulled out a dress. I realized it was the one she'd been wearing the night before, one of her late sister's. But now, pinned to the breast, was a brooch in the shape of a rose which I had never seen before. Mrs. Cotton stared at it, as though doubting its very existence.

"I shall get to the bottom of this!" she said, then strode out of the room, hauling the garment with her.

I didn't understand what the fuss was about, but as I was brushing a cobweb from the picture rail I noticed that there was a scuffed footprint on the inside of the windowsill. It was faint, but definitely there. Someone had climbed into the room from the outside.

I took my cloth to wipe the mark away.

Six

It was only after Lizzy and I had gathered up the dirty laundry that I found out my suspicions were correct. The housekeeper had us lined up in the hallway —me, Rob, Lizzy and Cook. Mr. Lock looked on, as though unsure whether he was to join our group or not. Strictly speaking, he didn't fall under Mrs. Cotton's rule, but she seemed to exert her power over him regardless. She was holding the brooch in her hand.

"I put a great deal of faith in you," she began, "and one of you has let me down. One of you entered my poor dead sister's private room and meddled with her property."

I dared not look at any of the others; Mrs. Cotton's eyes held us in our place like moths on pins.

She fixed me with the longest stare, as though trying to wring an admission out of me. "When I find out who was responsible, there will be consequences," she said. "Now, back to work."

As soon as she had gone, Mr. Lock shook his head and ambled off to polish the silver. Cook said something under her breath about "children's games," and Rob winked at me.

On the stairs, I tapped him on the shoulder. "You need to be more careful, Mr. Willmett," I said. "You left a mark as clear as day. She might have seen."

"Did I?" he said, shrugging. "She was too busy running from the room chased by Lady Greave's ghost, I reckon."

"How did you do it?" I said. "Get up there, I mean."

"Simple," he said. "Mr. Lock asked me to clean the gutters, and I took a ladder up the back of the house. I was in and out in less than a minute. Found the brooch in the jewelry box, fixed it to the dress Mrs. Cotton was wearing for New Year's Eve."

"Rob, you are *wicked*," I said. "Her face was a picture."

"Well, I'll not have her making your life a misery without something to pay it back," said Rob. "And look at her, wearing Her Ladyship's clothes as though they were her own!"

We parted ways as Mr. Lock shambled past with the

post. Life at Greave Hall was always like this. Starved of contact, we snatched conversation when we could. But what Rob said was true. And it wasn't just the clothes and jewelry. With Lord Greave confined to his bed more and more, Mrs. Cotton had even taken to having friends round for dinner once or twice a week, treating the house like her own. More than once Rob had asked Mr. Lock where it would stop, and if His Lordship even knew what was going on. The butler, ever proper, had told him to mind his own business.

Come back soon, Sammy, I thought.

Lord Greave came back to the Hall at about six o'clock, his face lined with worry and leaning heavily on his stick. Mrs. Cotton announced that they'd take their dinner together, and an hour later, preceded by Mr. Lock, His Lordship came down the stairs dressed in his jacket and tie. He had even shaved. Mrs. Cotton was wearing one of her sister's better dresses, but her bloodless lips were pressed into a scowl.

The kitchen was hot, with Cook bustling around the roasting jack. A joint of mutton dripped into the gravy tray, and Rowena lay stretched out beside the doorway. With her stomach swelled so large, it couldn't be long.

"Abi, peel us some carrots, will you?" said Cook.

I set to work, my mouth watering at the rich scents of the food. There'd likely be at least some broth for us later, made from the leftovers.

"His Lordship wants a celebration," muttered Cook. "Well, it's a celebration he shall have."

"Has there been more news of Samuel then?" I asked.

"Only that he's expected in two days' time," said Cook, "and that he was wounded in an act of bravery that saved the lives of many men."

I felt as proud as if he really were my brother. Lord Greave had always wanted his son to follow him into the navy, but from a young age Samuel was obsessed with toy soldiers. They still stood on a little shelf in the nursery, waiting for him to return.

I went up to my room after finishing scrubbing the pans, my arms aching from all the carrying up and down the stairs. I was getting ready for bed when Lizzy poked her head round the door. "It's freezing," she said. "Can I come in with you tonight?"

We'd often share on cold nights, and thought nothing of it. Better that than never get warm.

I said she could and we slipped under the sheets. She was chattering away about Henry, a footman who worked for Lord Greave's friends, the Ambroses; she'd seen him in the Park walking their mastiff, Pericles, and had waved, but apparently he hadn't waved back. I must have been quieter than normal because she suddenly broke off and asked if I was all right.

"Just tired," I said. In fact, I was more exhausted than I remembered being in a long while. Perhaps it was all the talk of Samuel returning, or the night of my attempted escape catching up with me, but I barely had the strength to blow out the candle beside the bed.

"We got Mrs. Cotton back, didn't we, Abi?" Lizzy said. "I kept lookout while Rob went up the ladder."

I chuckled. "It was very clever, but you mustn't do it for me. I don't want you all getting into trouble on my account."

"We've got to stick together," said Lizzy. She squeezed my arm. "We heard her squeal from the scullery. Rob reckons she actually believes there is a ghost. Caught her asking Mr. Lock if he'd seen anything unusual in the house. She won't even look at the picture on the stairs!"

"I'm only saying we need to be careful," I said. "Mustn't push it too far."

Lizzy giggled, then continued talking about the footman. "With Samuel back, Alexander Ambrose might be coming over again," she said. "And if Alexander comes, then he'll probably bring Henry with him . . ."

I wasn't really listening and must have fallen asleep, because I woke some time later. The clock was chiming a distant midnight.

Beneath the bedclothes, I shivered. A breeze was tickling my face.

Strange, I thought. The window must be open.

Had Lizzy opened it to let in some air? She was lying with her back to me, her body cocooned in warm sleep. I was annoyed. It was hard enough sleeping in a room without a fire—why did she have to go and let in more cold air?

I swung my legs out of bed and my bare feet found the floorboards. Rubbing my eyes, I saw that the window wasn't open only a crack, but a full arm's length. The threadbare drapes fluttered. On a January night, indeed! We'd be lucky not to catch pneumonia. What was she thinking?

I considered waking her, but then thought better of

it. She'd been so kind since she'd got back. There was no need to start on her over a careless act. I crossed the room and put my hands to the top of the sash, pulling down.

The window seemed stuck. However hard I tugged, it wouldn't close. I looked across at Lizzy, about to ask for her help, when all of a sudden a gust blew into the room, wrapping me in a cold embrace.

Something colder still tightened on my wrist.

I turned back to the window.

A hand, knuckles white as bone and streaked with dirt, gripped my arm. I saw nails, jagged and broken, as if the person had been clawing at the ground, and the long fingers pressed into my skin. My eyes followed the the cords of a starved wrist and a forearm lined with purple veins. There was a face there too—just a shadow in the darkness and the glint of an eye.

I screamed and pulled away, stumbling backwards and crashing into the wall behind. For a moment the fingers of the hand stretched out. I knew, as well as I knew my own mind, that it wanted to latch on to something in the room—to grasp me again.

I watched the fingers flexing, unable to breathe or speak.

Slowly the hand withdrew into the darkness.

Seven

LIZZY PUSHED OFF THE QUILT AND SAT UP.

"What? What is it?" She saw me on the floor. "Abi?"

My eyes were still on the black rectangle of the window, expecting that at any moment the hand would reappear. "There!" I said, pointing a trembling finger.

Lizzy got out of bed slowly, looking from the open window back to me. "Abi, why did you open the window? We'll catch our death."

"I didn't. You did. You opened it."

Lizzy frowned and crouched beside me. "It wasn't me, Abi. Why would I do such a thing?"

There was a creak of footsteps outside the door. We both knew whose. Lizzy flew across the room and pulled down the sash. She took my hand and dragged me back to the bed as the door was pushed open. Mrs. Cotton stood there, dressed in her nightgown.

"What is the meaning of this noise?" she asked. "It's past midnight and the decent folk of this household are trying to sleep."

"Just a nightmare, ma'am," said Lizzy quickly. "Sorry for the disturbance."

Mrs. Cotton cast her eyes across the room and I saw her shiver, for it was still perishing. She gestured to Lizzy. "What's she doing in here?"

"Just trying to keep warm, ma'am," said Lizzy.

"Get back to your own room," said Mrs. Cotton. "And no more of this. You'll wake the dead with your racket."

She turned and seemed to float back along the corridor, the only sound her nightdress brushing the floorboards.

"Thank you," I said to Lizzy. Her quick thinking had saved us from punishment, for sure. My mind was still reeling.

"What was the matter?" she asked. "Why were you on the floor?"

I was quiet for a moment, trying to work out what I'd seen. We were three storeys above the ground, yet there had been someone outside the window. I hadn't opened it, had I? Unless I somehow did so in my sleep, and the hand had been part of a dream. Perhaps that was possible. After all, my sleep had been plagued with terrors many times over the past year.

"You're right," I said, confused. "It must have been a nightmare."

Lizzy wrapped her arms around me from behind, and I was grateful to have someone close. She soon fell asleep again, but it took me much longer. I could still see that hideous hand in my sleep, the nails caked in grime, the fingers grasping . . .

But worse than that, in the pale light, I was sure I could still see the red bands they had left round my wrist.

❦

The following morning, as I tended to the fires, I tried to keep my mind on other things, but it kept going back to what I thought I'd seen. By the time the sun was slanting into the drawing room, I genuinely believed it had been a dream after all. If there had ever been marks on my wrist, they were gone now.

"Sleep well, m'lady?" Rob asked as I helped Cook to prepare breakfast for Lord Greave and Mrs. Cotton. It was an innocent question, and one he would ask most mornings. But for some reason, perhaps lack of sleep, I found it grating that morning. He must have seen the dark shadows beneath my eyes.

"Not really," I said.

"Oh," he replied, then smiled. "No ghosts in the night?"

"What?" My tone was brisk.

It had been him! Of course it had! Somehow he had used the ladder again. He'd climbed the house outside in the dead of night, rubbed dirt into his hands. Why hadn't I seen it before?

I looked at him coldly and his smile vanished.

"I must look at getting Lancelot shod," he said quietly. "He threw one on Piccadilly yesterday, and Lord Greave said it wouldn't do."

He left the room and as soon as he was gone, I felt overcome by sadness. Mrs. Cotton was our enemy, not Rob. Lizzy said we should stick together, not taunt each other. I burnt the first slice of His Lordship's toast and had to make another. Rowena was happy though. Even burnt toast was better than none.

The morning had passed without incident. It was laundry day—the worst of the week, when we took in all the sheets and linen and plunged them over and over in hot or cold water in the great laundry-room sinks. Any stains were scrubbed out with soaps, then sheets and tablecloths were passed through the mangle and smaller items wrung out. Hands went from numb with cold to scalding red. Wires were strung across the room for drying in winter, but Mrs. Cotton told us to air the sheets outside while the light was good and the skies clear.

"She seems a bit distracted, don't you think?" said Lizzy. "Why, she hasn't even lashed me with her tongue once today!"

After His Lordship's lunch, we found out why. We were enjoying the warmth from the range and eating cold cuts. Mr. Lock had told Cook that there was no need to prepare dinner for Lord Greave that evening, as he was visiting his club for the first time in several months.

This itself was big enough news: he'd all but given up going out to see acquaintances after Samuel had shipped out, keeping more and more to his rooms. Cook continued as she returned a pan to its station, "Mrs. Cotton has a visitor, though, and will be entertaining him in the drawing room."

We all looked up. The housekeeper having visitors

was not especially surprising, but mostly these were other ladies. And this didn't sound like a dinner party.

"*Him?*" I said.

"Indeed," said Cook.

"A single gentleman?" said Lizzy.

"So Mr. Lock says," said Cook.

"Well, who is he?" said Rob.

Cook only shrugged.

We continued with our duties separately that afternoon, but I think we all must have been thinking the same thing. Who was this strange gentleman, and what was his business with our housekeeper? The thought that he might be a suitor of some sort seemed close to ridiculous. There was a rumor of Mrs. Cotton once being in a relationship, an engagement called off. Surely no man could endure her!

The fact that this man was calling when Lord Greave was not at home added to our suspicions. I doubted the master of the house even knew of the visit, and said as much to Lizzy.

At about four o'clock, when I was ironing the dried napkins and handkerchiefs—a job that seemed never-ending—Rob came up to me. He asked me first if I wouldn't mind cleaning his best set of boots, as Lizzy was busy upstairs. I said that I would get round to it, but then he lingered.

"How would you like to find out who our visitor is tonight?" he said.

"I don't think Mrs. Cotton is going to say," I replied.

"But if there was another way?" There was a mischievous glint in his eye.

"What are you up to?" I asked.

Rob outlined his plan to me, and my first impression was that it was plain madness. "Absolutely not," I said. He wouldn't drop it though, and as I polished his shoes to a shine he pressed on, meeting each of my very sensible objections with a clever answer. He and Elizabeth had thought of each eventuality, he said.

"So Lizzy's in on this too, is she?"

"Even Cook's agreed!" he said. "But none of it will work without you."

There was a part of me, too, that wanted to get Mrs. Cotton back. And breaking the rules was the only way.

I nodded reluctantly.

"Is that a yes?" Rob asked.

"I'll do it," I said.

Eight

I DIDN'T HAVE TIME TO DWELL ON MY DECISION, for the rest of the day passed quickly. Lord Greave left at six, and I went up to clean his room. The curtains of the bed were drawn and the room smelled of age and decay. The sheets were changed once a week, normally, but he had insisted on keeping these for four times as long. Up here there were more pictures—hunting scenes and an oil of the naval battle at Trafalgar, where His Lordship's father had fought and died—and a bureau, now little used if the gathering dust was anything to go by.

I swept away the ashes of his fire and made it ready to be lit the following morning. I brushed away a cobweb that had appeared in the corner of the slanted wall, then cleaned the carpets and the inside of the windows, and polished the dressing table and mirror. There were clothes to put away too, and I left them on the bed while

I saw to His Lordship's separate water closet. I cleaned the porcelain sink, making sure each surface sparkled.

I was scrubbing the water closet floor with a rough cloth when I was struck with the overwhelming impression that someone had entered the room at my back.

"I'll put away the clothes shortly," I said, thinking it could only be Mr. Lock.

When no one answered, I stood up and went back into the bedroom. Someone had closed the curtains around the bed.

"Mr. Lock?" I said.

No response.

"Rob?" I whispered.

The bedroom door, I noticed, was closed. I had left it open to let in some fresher air.

"Robert Willmett," I said more loudly, "your notion of fun is not the same as mine."

The curtains didn't move, but I couldn't help but feel there was someone lurking behind them.

I scolded myself for being foolish. I felt like dashing straight out of the door as fast as my feet could carry me, but instead I crept to the bed. Taking a deep breath, I yanked the curtain aside.

The bed was empty, neatly made up as I'd left it, but the clothes were gone.

I ran out on to the landing, expecting to see Rob or Lizzy laughing, or perhaps Mr. Lock stiffly descending the stairs. My back had been turned for a minute at most, and in that time someone had been into the room, taken the clothes and pulled the bed curtains closed, all in absolute silence.

Someone was playing games with me. Not Mr. Lock, certainly. He wasn't the sort. Not Rob, who was out with His Lordship. Lizzy then? But that made no sense: why would she break our trust? I went into the dressing room, and sure enough, the shirts were hanging on a rail. A rug had been laid in here, but in the corner was a hatch. It opened into the nursery below, but as I knew it hadn't been opened for years.

I told myself I was being silly.

As we weren't preparing a dinner for His Lordship, we managed half an hour to eat our own. Once Mr. Lock had gone to his own bed for an early night, Rob said to me: "No second thoughts, then, Abi? Still game?"

I wasn't, but I nodded. Truth be told, I was as curious as any of them as to who Mrs. Cotton's guest might be.

"Good," Lizzy said. "We'll get to the bottom of it, for sure."

"I'll ring the bell when I see him come off the road," said Rob. "Lizzy, that's your signal to distract Mrs. Cotton, and yours Abi, to be ready."

I occupied myself with needlework in my room, repairing a seat cushion, while Lizzy helped Cook clear up downstairs. What would my mother say if she knew about this eavesdropping? She wouldn't approve, I was sure of it. But Rob was right—as long as I didn't make any noise, there was little reason why I should get caught. And there was no denying that I felt excited.

When your life's governed so strictly by rules, breaking even the smallest ones gives a thrill of satisfaction.

As the hours went by I began to wonder if this guest would come at all, but at close to ten the little bell in my room rang. That was my signal that Rob had spotted the visitor coming off the road. I was on my feet and down the two flights of stairs as quickly as I could manage.

Lizzy winked at me as she emerged from the back stairs and went to the drawing room. Rapping twice, she said, "Ma'am, could Cook have a quick word downstairs?"

"Can't it wait?" said Mrs. Cotton irritably. "My visitor will be here shortly."

"She says it's urgent, ma'am."

"Oh, very well," said Mrs. Cotton.

I hung back as their footsteps went towards the scullery. Just then, the doorbell chimed.

I held my breath. If Mrs. Cotton turned round now, the plan was ruined.

"Rob," she called, "escort our guest into the sitting room, please."

My heart was knocking under my ribs.

"Yes, ma'am," said Rob. As the shadows of Mrs. Cotton and Lizzy passed down into the scullery, I tiptoed out behind Rob. He was walking to the front door and gave me a wicked grin. I slipped into the sitting room.

The fire was banked high in the grate and all the lamps were lit, making the room warm and inviting. I moved quickly behind the painted screen on the other side of the room as a voice came from the hall.

"Good evening. My name is Doctor Matthias Reinhardt," a man said in a strange accent. "I'm here to see Mrs. Lillian Cotton."

A doctor? Was Mrs. Cotton ill? The thought gave me a little thrill, but it came with a flash of shame too.

If she was suffering from a secret ailment, then I really shouldn't be listening in.

"Of course, sir," said Rob. "Let me take your coat, doctor. If you'd like to follow me."

I wondered how the plan was going downstairs. By now Cook would have been admonished, no doubt, for interrupting the housekeeper with trivialities about the fish delivery and Mrs. Cotton would be huffing and puffing her way back upstairs.

With my eye up against the crack in the screen I saw a tall, grey-haired gentleman with a monocle enter the room behind Rob. He was dressed in a black suit with an odd little purple waistcoat and carried a satchel.

A moment later, Mrs. Cotton bustled in behind him.

"Good evening, Dr. Reinhardt. My apologies for being indisposed. With a house such as this to run, one has to deal with all sorts of problems"—here she grimaced at Rob—"not least of which are the staff."

It was his cue to leave, and he withdrew with the faintest of glances towards the screen, closing the door behind him.

Now it's just the three of us, I thought.

"And a good evening to you also, Mrs. Cotton," said the doctor. "May I say, from what I have seen, this is a most impressive house."

"It gives me small pleasure to know that I can preserve it in the state that my late sister would admire," said Mrs. Cotton, flushing a little.

"Yes," said the doctor. "And it is she about whom you contacted me, is it not? Eleanor."

Mrs. Cotton gave a small twitch. "You must think me a fool, doctor. Eleanor has been dead for nineteen—"

"Please," said the doctor, raising his palms to interrupt her. "There is no folly in what you have told me. Just because the body dies, that does not mean the spirit ceases to exist. A spirit must find its rest."

Mrs. Cotton smiled and gestured to a seat. "Will you take a drink of anything, doctor? Some whiskey, perhaps."

Who was this man? Not a doctor like Dr. Ingle, that much was certain.

"Oh, no thank you," he said, resting his bag beside the chair. "I find that such things . . . how can I say? . . . disrupt the energies."

I had no idea what he was talking about, of course. So this had something to do with His Lordship's late wife, Eleanor.

Mrs. Cotton poured herself a drink instead.

"Shall we begin, then?" asked the visitor.

Mrs. Cotton took a small sip. "Very well."

"You did what I asked? Fetched one of her possessions?"

Mrs. Cotton went to the handsome dresser and pulled open the drawer. She took something out and held it out before the doctor. I pressed closer still to see.

The rose-shaped brooch.

"This was her favorite," she said.

I almost laughed. So this was about Rob's little trick! I thought Mrs. Cotton might go on to mention how it had mysteriously appeared on the dress, but she fell silent.

Oh, you stupid woman! I was already looking forward to telling the others. This was better than any of us could have imagined!

"Most attractive!" said the doctor. He laid the brooch carefully on the low table. The housekeeper sat opposite the doctor, with her hands clasped between her knees.

"Can you tell me, Mrs. Cotton," said Dr. Reinhardt, "what your sister liked to be called? Was it Eleanor, or something shorter? Elle, perhaps?"

"I called her Ellie."

The doctor smiled. "Ellie. That's good. And can you tell me, madam, have you any notion why your sister might still be here? Why she might be . . . pestering you so?"

I had to clasp my hand over my mouth. Mrs. Cotton seriously believed that Lady Greave's spirit was haunting her!

"I have no idea," said Mrs. Cotton. "It's been so long, and we were always close."

Dr. Reinhardt nodded appreciatively and put two fingers on the brooch, closing his eyes for a few seconds. He held out his other hand to the housekeeper. "Please, madam, to commune with the dead we must form a link of flesh and blood."

Hesitantly, Mrs. Cotton reached out her hands and took the doctor's. She too closed her eyes. I kept mine wide open. I didn't want to miss a second. I imagined Rob and Lizzy rolling around on the floor laughing when I told them.

"You too must touch the token," said the doctor. "Complete the bonds."

Mrs. Cotton did as he said. She looked so baffled and unsure, not at all her usual self.

The only sound now was the crackle of the fire.

Who was this "doctor"? Some sort of mountebank, surely, willing to take money from anyone gullible enough to be parted from it. I hated Mrs. Cotton, but

I'd never thought her a fool.

The doctor turned his head towards the screen and looked straight at me. "I know you're here," he whispered.

I stepped back from the crack in the screen. Panic flooded my limbs.

"Reveal yourself!" commanded the doctor.

Nine

ALL THE LAUGHTER LEFT ME AS FEAR TOOK OVER. I was sure that any moment Mrs. Cotton would step behind the screen and drag me out. I couldn't imagine what punishment she would devise. And could I conceal the fact that Rob and Lizzie were part of the plan too? Mrs. Cotton must surely see that my presence was orchestrated by several people.

"I say again, troubled one, reveal yourself."

His voice was softer this time, and still Mrs. Cotton hadn't said anything. With my heart thudding, I crept back to the screen and peered through.

They were seated just as before, their eyes still closed and hands clasped. Neither was even looking in my direction, but Dr. Reinhardt's face was tensed, his jaw muscles tight lines under the skin.

"Ellie," whispered the doctor, "come forth. Explain yourself."

Relief flooded over me, drowning my panic.

Then, from somewhere there came a draft. One of the lamps flickered. Mrs. Cotton's eyes opened in alarm then closed again. I looked at the windows, but both were closed with the curtains drawn.

"Ellie," said the doctor calmly, "we are your friends."

If he was playing a trick, he was quite an actor. There was nothing overly dramatic in his voice. He spoke as if to an old acquaintance, warm and faintly mocking.

Something in the room had changed, however. The darkness seemed to have deepened, as though someone had dimmed the lamps.

"Ellie?" asked Mrs. Cotton, as the light played across her hard features.

"No," said Dr. Reinhardt anxiously. "Not her. Not Ellie."

He had been sitting up straight before, but suddenly he tipped his head, lowering his chin to his chest. It was as though he was drifting into sleep.

Mrs. Cotton opened her eyes. "Doctor? What do you mean, not Ellie?"

The doctor didn't reply. I couldn't see his face clearly, but I thought that in the shadows his lips were moving.

"Ow!" said Mrs. Cotton. "You're hurting me, Doctor."

She tried to pull her hand away, and I could see that the doctor's fingers had hers in a tight grip. The rest of his body was motionless.

"Doctor!" she cried. "I must insist—"

He suddenly released her hand and she fell back in the chair, pale with shock. As she did so the fire in the grate went out, not with a slow fizzle but suddenly, as though the chimney had swallowed it. One moment it was blazing high, the next it was gone.

I gasped, and if Mrs. Cotton had not done so in the same instant, I would have given myself away. The room was suddenly cold.

Only the oil lamps were now lit. Gooseflesh rose across my skin.

The doctor began to move again. Both hands seemed to slither back to his chair, and his knuckles whitened as he clutched the armrests. His head lifted slowly, and even in the gloom I could see that his eyes were rolled back, showing the whites.

I thought he was having some sort of fit. His lips were drawn back over his teeth and his head turned jerkily to left and right.

"Doctor?" said Mrs. Cotton. She was shifting in her

seat, casting glances into the corners of the room.

When the doctor spoke, the voice was not his own. It was an unearthly moan that seemed to rise from the pit of his stomach. He spoke a single word in a wail of desperation. The word was "Murder!"

Mrs. Cotton's face was a mask of horror. Her mouth moved as though she were trying to speak, but couldn't. My attention was quickly drawn back to the chair. Dr. Reinhardt had started to shake. I could hear his teeth rattling.

"Doctor?" said Mrs. Cotton again.

A white foam began to bubble on the man's lips, flecking his chin and dripping in clots on to his waist-coat. Mrs. Cotton rose from her seat as a monotone growl rumbled from his mouth, and the arms of the chair creaked as he strained against it.

"I'll fetch help," she said, crossing the room in a flurry. "I'll come back."

She rushed from the room, and now there were only two of us.

What was I to do? Stay put or run? If I was caught leaving the room . . . It didn't bear thinking about.

A series of sharp convulsions gripped the doctor's body and on the last, the chair toppled sideways. He landed like a sack of coal, upturning a side table and sending a lamp crashing over.

I rushed to his side. Blood trickled from his nose. Whether this was caused by the strength of the seizure or a blow to the head when he fell, I didn't know. His pupils were visible again, but dilated.

"Doctor Reinhardt?" I said. "Can you hear me?"

His pupils focused suddenly and his gaze locked on mine. Fear tightened his brow, but there was something else. Bewilderment isn't the right word, nor sadness.

He looked at me with recognition.

Tears made his eyes suddenly glassy, and he reached up slowly. I don't know why I didn't shrink away as he touched my cheek, his hand smooth and warm.

"Little Snowdrop," he said.

My face was suddenly hot. I thought I must have misheard.

"My Snowdrop," he said again and this time there was no mistaking it.

"You must leave here," he said.

The word on my lips found its sound. "Mama?"

It will sound foolish to you, of course, but through the sheen of sweat and the bloodied aquiline nose, through the jaw matted with the shadow of a beard, past the narrow lips, through his brown eyes—through all these things, so unlike my mother, I swear, as God is my witness, that I saw her.

There were footsteps on the stairs. Not long now.

"What do you mean?" I asked.

"Murdered, Abi. You—"

"Stand away, Abi," said Rob. The doctor's hand fell limply from my cheek and suddenly the room was a bustle of people. I was brushed aside as Rob knelt beside the stricken doctor, loosening his tie and cradling his head. Lizzy stood back and Mrs. Cotton hovered near the door, fingering the collar of her dress nervously. If she noticed I was there, she showed no sign of being suspicious. Her eyes were on the doctor.

"Get me some brandy, Elizabeth," said Rob. "Come now, sir," he said to the doctor, slapping his cheek gently. "Let's see you well."

As Lizzy busied herself with the drink, Dr. Reinhardt stirred. His hand drifted to his nose. "Where on earth? What? Oh dear!"

"Easy does it," said Rob, propping the doctor up against the chair. "You had a turn, sir. Nothing more. Better now. Take it slow."

The doctor accepted the proffered brandy glass in a trembling hand and took a slow sip. His eyes travelled ashamedly across each of us in turn. "I assure you," he said, with a measure of composure, "this has never happened before."

I searched his gaze for any sign of what was there before, but it was gone. Before me, sitting on the carpet, was a middle-aged man. Nothing more. Whatever spirit had possessed him had left.

Ten

My hands were shaking so much I thrust them beneath my apron so that no one would see.

The doctor had asked for a second "restorative" following his first, and had almost finished that ten minutes later. The room had been righted and I had fetched a brush to sweep up the broken glass from the fallen lamp. Normally the thought of getting oil out of the carpet would have filled me with despair, but I was glad to be out of the room if only for a moment.

"What can you remember?" Rob asked.

"I recall entering the room," said the doctor, "and my conversation with Mrs. Cotton about . . ."

From my knees on the rug, I caught the glance from the housekeeper that silenced him.

" . . . yes, but then nothing. I must have been unconscious after I hit my head."

Rob and Lizzy both looked at Mrs. Cotton expectantly, but she too had regained her composure and her brusque demeanor. "I went to find help as soon as I saw the beginnings of your attack, Doctor. Like you, I am at a loss to explain it."

Lizzy stoked the fire. I could see from the corner of my eye that she was trying to catch my attention, but I daren't look up for fear of what she would see in my face. I needed time to think.

Doctor Reinhardt finished his drink and placed the glass on the table.

"Well, it's late," said Mrs. Cotton, "and I'm sure you will not want to be detained any longer, Doctor. Robert? The doctor's coat, please."

Dr. Reinhardt nodded. Even if he wasn't ready to leave, Mrs. Cotton's tone implied no invitation to linger. He stood stiffly, gathering up his bag.

"If you require my services again, madam, you have my details."

Mrs. Cotton replied that she had, and left the room with a brief farewell. The doctor paid no attention at all to me as he followed her out into the hallway. Why should he? I was a girl, an insignificant member of a household. A layer of fires, a scrubber of saucepans, a sweeper of rooms.

But to me he was everything. He had opened a door into a room I had thought locked twelve months before. I wanted more than anything to stop him, question him further, but I couldn't. Even to put a hand on his arm would have been deemed improper.

And so I watched as Rob closed the door on him and the doctor slipped from my life, taking with him the key to the closed door—the door to my mother.

"Well," whispered Rob, running a hand across his forehead in mock relief. "What happened?"

His eagerness irritated me. "Not now," I said crossly, turning to the stairs. He caught up with me and placed his hand on my shoulder.

"Abi, what's the matter?"

His smile had gone. Some can cloak their feelings, but not Rob. His face had no means of dissembling, and I could see I'd hurt him. "It's nothing," I said. "Let's talk in the morning. I'm tired, that's all."

He nodded and wished me goodnight.

"At least tomorrow is a day of rest."

Normally I would have laughed at our private joke. Sunday was only a fraction less toilsome than the rest of the week, in that we were given time off after lunch for ourselves. Unless, that is, Mrs. Cotton devised some tasks for us. She herself would visit the church in the morning, returning to take dinner with her brother-in-law. Lizzy, now seventeen, was permitted to venture out alone in the afternoon, but I was not. After my failed escape, I doubted I would be allowed outside unchaperoned ever again.

I lay awake for yet another night. *My Snowdrop*, he had called me. It couldn't be a coincidence. I briefly considered that it might have been a trick Mrs. Cotton was playing, but that was too unlikely. She might have heard the name my mother used for me, but not even she would go to such lengths to torture me.

What other explanation could there be for the events of that evening?

The doctor had called me "Abi" too, and we had of course not been introduced. And why had he stopped speaking when the others came into the room, unless the message was meant only for me?

I had heard of mediums before. My mother had been a woman with no time for nonsense, and she had spoken of them in the same breath as con men or pickpockets. Yet she had chosen to use one of them as a way to reach me.

My mother had died of cholera, like so many others in the previous year. I forced myself to remember her final days.

From the moment she first fell ill, complaining of cramps in her stomach, Mrs. Cotton had refused to enter the room for fear that the stench would somehow pass to her. So it was left to me to tend to my mother, carrying out the pails of waste her body rejected, and taking in water by the gallon to meet her unquenchable thirst. Through her tears she had told me that she burned inside. After a day, her violent retching had given way to silent spasms that shook her body and made her whole body damp with sweat. The doctor had said there was nothing to be done but keep her comfortable until the illness either passed or took her with it. In the early morning it had done the latter. She seemed in an hour to become an old woman, her flesh shrinking across her bones, her lips turning the blue of violets. She died at seventeen minutes past four according to my father's watch.

That wasn't murder, unless . . .

"Poison."

The word leapt to my lips without me thinking. But it made perfect sense. Only poison could have looked like cholera.

One thing was clear. I could tell no one of what Dr. Reinhardt had said. Not yet. They would think that I was out of my mind. After the scare in His Lordship's bedroom and the hand at the window, perhaps I was.

I knew, of course, that there could be no murder without motive, and in the early hours I lay awake wondering what possible reason there could be to kill my mother. Who could harbor such hatred towards such a gentle soul?

My mind reached for a name, but I could hardly countenance it. Mrs. Cotton was such a God-fearing woman and the act itself so monstrous. She and my mother had hardly seen eye to eye, but to call that a motive for murder was a step too far.

Unless she was more diabolical than I'd ever imagined.

Eleven

THE NOTE THAT ARRIVED AFTER BREAKFAST made
me forget for a moment at least about murder and
poison. It didn't take long for the news to filter through
the house while Mrs. Cotton was at church. Samuel was
at Portsmouth, and being transferred to London.

"He will be with us tomorrow," said Cook.

Rob was sent to notify Dr. Ingle. The mention of
his name made me turn from the dishes I was washing.
Dr. Ingle had come to certify my mother's death,
though his arrival had been delayed as he was busy
with wealthier patrons. I had often wondered whether
the outcome might have been different if he had come
sooner. It occurred to me, for the first time, that his visit
had been a quick one. He had been and gone within
ten minutes, enough time to give the body a cursory
examination only.

So who had diagnosed my mother's condition?

The cholera was rife at the time, the papers full of it. It was well known that the only way to bring respite to the patient was to give them as much water as possible. But what if we had all been laboring under a misapprehension?

My skin began to tingle. The doubts I had about Dr. Reinhardt's strange words were falling away. If it wasn't cholera, then was it such a leap to poison and murder?

Upstairs, Elizabeth was brushing her hair while I changed into my cleaning dress.

"Lizzy," I said. "You remember my mother's death?"

She paused a moment, then put down her brush and came over to me.

"I'm so sorry, Abi. It's a year since, isn't it?"

"Near enough," I said. "I've been thinking about it."

Elizabeth, along with me, had taken her turn at nursing my mother through her final hours, fetching water and thin soup and changing the soiled sheets.

"You shouldn't, Abi," she said, holding my shoulders to face her.

"How did we know it was cholera she suffered from?" I asked.

A frown crinkled Lizzy's forehead. "Well, what else could it have been?"

"It wasn't Dr. Ingle who said so, was it?"

"Abi, I don't understand," she said, turning away. "There's nothing to be done now, is there?"

I held my tongue. I should have told her then about Dr. Reinhardt's message, but doubted myself still—I was getting carried away.

She must have mistaken my silence for grief. She looked at me again, framed by the window.

"Those that died are in a better place, Abi," she said. There was a tear in her eye.

I cursed myself silently. One of Elizabeth's two sisters had been carried off by cholera a few months before my mother and Lizzy had thought at the time that she had brought the sickness into her house—Mrs. Cotton said as much. Later, though, it was said to be something in the water—or so the papers claimed.

"Silly me," I said. "I'm sorry to go on, Lizzy."

"It's fine," said Lizzy, wiping her eyes. "Now, how do I look?"

"You look lovely," I said. She always did on a Sunday, but it wasn't the Almighty she was dressing up for, I guessed. "Are you seeing Henry later?"

His name brought a blush to her cheek.

"I am," she said. "He's promised me a gift."

"Then I hope it is a fine one," I said, giggling.

According to Lizzy, she and Henry had met one Sunday at the local church, the September before last, when he had offered her a ride home. She had asked him if his employer would not object, for it was hardly a servant's place in the back of such a handsome carriage, and he had replied that it wasn't half handsome enough for her. I'd rolled my eyes at his easy flattery, but since then Elizabeth seemed to look forward to her Sunday outings more and more.

"If Mr. Ambrose sees you flirting with his foot-man," I said, "word will get back to Mrs. Cotton. You know she won't countenance it."

Elizabeth dusted a little rouge onto her cheeks and rubbed it in, checking her reflection in a hand-held mirror.

"I had better be careful then," she grinned. "Wish me luck."

"Good luck," I said, "and do be careful."

She skipped out and down the stairs, and I couldn't help but smile. There weren't many places to find happiness at Greave Hall, and Lizzy deserved hers, but she knew as well as I that Mrs. Cotton had dismissed the previous parlor maid, Anne, when she discovered her with a follower. The man in question was a clerk from an office in the city, my mother told me. Well-to-do in most respects, but when he'd been found lurking by the back door after curfew, it was the last we saw of Anne.

As we suspected, there was little rest that Sunday. Mr. Lock was out running errands with His Lordship and Rob while I was set to ironing Samuel's freshly laundered clothes. It was a labor heating up the irons against the stove one at a time, then holding them with a cloth to protect my hands.

Cook was bustling to and fro, taking stock and planning the meals for the week ahead. While I came to fetch another iron, she emerged from the pantry and added something to her list.

There was something I needed to ask her.

"Miss McMahon," I said.

"Hm?" she grunted.

"The other night, when I tried . . . you know . . ."

"Better if you had," said Cook. "One less mouth to feed."

I had learned not to expect any outward show of affection from her. My mother told me that after her husband, a tanner, had died, she was forced into service because she could no longer pay the rent of her home. She had children somewhere.

Despite her gruff manner I knew she cared a little,

for she would sometimes allow me a dip of honey on my bread when Mrs. Cotton wasn't looking on. Her kindnesses were small ones, rationed out like sugar.

"Did you draw the bolt on the coal door?" I said pointing through to the scullery.

"Bolt?" she said. "I did no such thing, child. Why should I?"

"I thought you might have done it to help me. You see, that's the way I went out."

"Well then, you are to blame for any bolt, my girl."

"You don't understand," I said. "I didn't put the bolt back across."

Cook waved her hand as if to shoo me away. "I haven't got time for talk of bolts now, Abi. Must have been Robert, or that Elizabeth."

"But it wasn't them," I said.

"Mary, mother of God!" she gasped. "It must have been Rowena then!"

The cat lifted her nose at the sound of her name, then settled once more.

Cook's anger took me by surprise and my hand slipped on the iron. I cried out as it burned me.

"Oh, you daft thing!" she tutted crossly, leading me over to the sink. She placed my hand in a bowl of cold water. Pain throbbed under the skin in time to my heartbeat.

Twelve

I STARCHED SAMUEL'S COLLARS AND TOOK HIS
shirts and other clothes into his new room in the library,
placing them carefully in the wardrobe that had been
carried down. It was hard to believe that he would soon
be home. Perhaps once he was better, I could find a way
to tell him about my suspicions.

A voice spoke behind me.

"There's no reason to linger, Miss Tamper."

Mrs. Cotton appeared in the door of the library,
hands clasped in front of her.

"No, ma'am," I said. "I was just—"

"Just being idle," said Mrs. Cotton. "The windows
need washing. When you've done so, bring Master
Greave's mirror down, along with his shaving brushes
and razor. Set them on the nightstand."

"Very well, ma'am."

I went to the door, but Mrs. Cotton did not step aside to let me pass. Her body seemed to suck the heat from the air, so that being close to her brought a chill over my skin. She reached out and put a hand under my chin, pulling my face up to meet her gaze.

"This changes nothing, you know," she said.

I swallowed. Did she know somehow of what Dr. Reinhardt had said?

I must have looked blank.

"The return of Master Greave," she went on, "will change nothing."

I nodded quickly. "Of course, ma'am."

"I would advise you, Miss Tamper, to remember your place."

In the kitchen I filled a pail with water and soap, and found clean cloths for the windows. I knew Mrs. Cotton would inspect later on, so there were no short cuts. First I soaped the dirt from the coal fires from the glass, then I wiped away the smears with a damp cloth, finally drying them. I had to stand on a stool to reach the tops.

I was washing the dining-room windows when Lord Greave's carriage rattled up outside. Mr. Lock helped him down and they came to the front door, side by side. Mr. Lock walked as he always did, bent over with his hands behind his back, nodding his head like a tired old crow. Rob caught sight of me watching from the window, and looked away. Whatever news there was, it seemed grave. He twitched Lancelot's reins with a snap of his gloved hands and continued, turning the carriage towards the stable yard.

Having finished the family rooms, I took some clean water upstairs to the attic, and was in my bedroom at the top of the house giving the glass a final rinse when Lizzy came in. Her face was ruddy with the cold outside, and she threw off her bonnet, rubbing her hands briskly together.

"Freezing out there," she said.

"Well?" I said.

"Well, what?" Lizzy asked, a smile growing on her face.

"Don't tease me," I said. "Was Henry there?" Lizzy sat on the bed and pulled out a length of material from the pouch in her dress. It was the most lovely blue scarf. The room seemed to light up in its presence.

"Looks expensive!" I said.

"Pure silk," said Lizzy, wrapping it round my neck. It felt like soft warm hands enfolding my skin, and I stroked the fabric against my cheek. Lizzy was beaming. But this was beyond the wages of a footman.

"Where did he get it?" I said.

"His master gave it to him," said Lizzy. "It was a gift for a lady, but there was a falling out. Mr. Ambrose didn't want it in the house."

I handed it back, as gently as if it were a living thing.

"It's beautiful," I said.

She played with the scarf in her lap and I could see she wanted to say something more. "Just spit it out," I said. "I need to take this water back down before Mrs. Cotton misses me."

"I kissed him," she said, not meeting my eyes.

"You didn't!"

She nodded. "I couldn't stop myself. On the cheek only!"

"Did anyone see you?"

"I don't think so," said Lizzy. "We were hidden by his master's carriage. It was very quick."

"Nevertheless . . ."

She screwed up her hands and brought her fists down on to the mattress. "I know—you don't have to tell me."

I obviously did. I couldn't have my only friend going the same way as Anne.

"Lizzy," I said, "you must break it off."

She looked at me with shock. "I can't do that."

"You must. He will expect the same again next time. Maybe more."

"Henry isn't like that," she said. "It was as much my fault as his."

"Well, even more reason to be cautious," I said.

Lizzy stood up and folded the scarf angrily.

"If I didn't know you better, Abi, I'd say you didn't want me to be happy."

"Don't be foolish!" I said. "And keep your voice down."

"Oh, I am a fool, now, am I?" she said. "Just because you're so miserable, it doesn't mean we all have to share your wretchedness."

She stormed out of the room, and I listened to her footsteps rattle along the corridor to her room.

I sighed. You're wrong, Lizzy, I thought. I wasn't jealous—at least not of Henry. How could I be? I'd never even laid eyes on him.

I picked up the pail and threw the cloth in, sloshing water over the sides.

But as I walked down the back stairs, I wondered if

maybe she wasn't right, at least a little. We both wanted to be away from Greave Hall and Mrs. Cotton. Perhaps Henry was a good sort, after all. And perhaps he was her ticket away from here.

There was one more set of windows to wash by four o'clock—Mrs. Cotton's. She kept her room locked at all times, and I found her in the drawing room, drinking tea from one of His Lordship's finest Worcester cups.

"I thought that I heard raised voices," she said, sipping delicately.

I replied that I didn't know what she could mean, but perhaps it was noise from the street. She didn't respond to that, but gave me the key to her bedroom.

"I shall expect it back shortly."

As I climbed the stairs with clean water, a plan formed in my mind. If I were to go through with it, I would have to be quick. If I was caught, my punishment would be unspeakable.

Mrs. Cotton's bedroom was immaculate. The bed looked like it hadn't been slept in, so neat were the sheets. I placed the bucket on the floor beside the window, and began to rub down the glass. It looked out over the road beyond and into the Park. Somewhere out there lived Dr. Reinhardt, and unless I was mistaken, somewhere in this room was the key to contacting him. I wiped while casting my eyes around. Apart from the bed, there was a wardrobe built into a recess beside the fireplace, a dressing table and a shelf above the bed which held a single book—her Bible. There was also a bureau.

No, Abi, I said to myself. Don't do this.

But it was my only chance.

I wrung out the cloth and pricked my ears for the slightest sound. If Mrs. Cotton were to come up the stairs, I told myself, I would hear her.

I crossed the room quickly and turned the small key that had been left in the lock of the writing-desk drawer. It opened. Inside was a pad of writing paper, some blotting pads and a collection of spare pen nibs. There was also a book bound in moleskin. I took it out.

It was an address book, the corners of the pages marked with the letters of the alphabet. My mouth was dry and my heart seemed to be thumping somewhere high in my throat as I skipped to R.

There were three entries on the page.

Rathbone, Frederick. 92 Silk Road
Reinhardt, Dr. M. 11b Argyle Terrace
Roberts, T. (chimneys and flues)
18 Kent Terrace

11b Argyle Terrace. It didn't sound like much, certainly not a grand place like Greave Hall. Probably a basement apartment by the sounds of it.

My ears caught the faint sound of rattling china. My fingers fumbled as I put the book back and closed the drawer.

The key wouldn't turn!

I tried again. No. It was jammed.

There were rapid footsteps on the stairs. Steps that could only be Mrs. Cotton's.

I pulled open the drawer and saw that the blotting pad was pushed up against the locking mechanism, so I moved it farther inside and closed the drawer again. This time it locked. I scurried quickly back to the window and snatched up the drying cloth. Behind me the door opened.

"Almost done, I hope," said Mrs. Cotton.

I didn't look around for fear she would read my guilt in my face.

"Yes, ma'am," I said. "Nearly there."

I felt her watch me for a while, and then, quiet as a fox, she was gone.

My heart took a long time to slow. Outside, the sun was already dipping to the west above the trees. Buckingham Palace was visible just beyond. The sky was awash with streaks of navy and orange. As I wiped back and forth, making sure no streaks remained, I chanted the address, making sure it was indelibly imprinted on my mind.

"11b Argyle Terrace. 11b Argyle Terrace. 11b Argyle Terrace."

I didn't know yet what I would do, but I knew one thing for certain: the basement apartment in Argyle Terrace held some answers.

Thirteen

I WENT DOWNSTAIRS TO EMPTY THE PAIL, AND
found that Cook had left—to find a tavern for the rest
of the night, no doubt, as she often did on a Sunday. I
needed paper, and it would be easiest to use the pad that
Cook and Lock used to write out her lists, but the store
beside his room was kept locked. Mrs. Cotton had a key,
of course, as did Mr. Lock. I decided to go to him.

Rob came in from outside, carrying an armful of logs.

"Looks like Rowena's time's come," he said. "She's
out there now in the stables, looking a sight sorry for
herself."

"Poor thing. Do you think she needs some food?"

"I daren't go near her," said Rob, grinning. "She gave
me a snarl like a Bengal tiger."

"I'll have a look," I said. "Do you know where Mr.
Lock is?" I asked.

He put the logs down beside the small woodburner in the kitchen. "With His Lordship, I think."

I thanked him, and took Rowena's bowl of water outside. The stable block was at the back of the yard. I clucked quietly as I entered, trying not to scare her.

There she was, lying at the back, on a tarpaulin. She lifted her head, then let it sink back when she saw it was only me.

"I bet you wanted to be away from all the fuss, didn't you?" I said, placing the bowl next to her head. She lapped gratefully at the water as I stroked her behind the ears. "Not long now, eh?"

She purred softly and gave a slow blink. "Well," I said, "this is what will happen if you get yourself a follower."

I left her, but I'd come back to check as often as possible. I didn't know what would happen to the kittens though. Perhaps Adam could take them to a good home. I had a feeling one cat was enough for Mrs. Cotton.

Back inside, I went in search of Mr. Lock. Rob was right—he was upstairs with His Lordship. But I could hardly go barging in, so I lurked impatiently near the bottom of the stairs, half-heartedly wiping the skirting with a cloth. I couldn't help hearing snatches of conversation, and realized they were speaking of Samuel.

". . . house isn't suitable for an invalid, Mr. Lock," said Lord Greave in a gruff voice.

I was shocked at how normal he sounded. So often now he spoke in gibberish or not at all. I felt a glimmer of hope.

"We have made the best of it, sir," said Mr. Lock. "The staff know their duties."

"Still, perhaps he would be better in a hospital," said His Lordship. "In some recuperative ward, where professionals can attend to him."

"Dr. Ingle will be here," said Mr. Lock. "And you heard what the staff sergeant said: Samuel wishes to return to his home."

I couldn't hear what His Lordship said next, and the butler emerged on to the stairs with His Lordship behind him. Though he was dressed smartly, his general demeanor was still wretched. His eyes were bloodshot, the lids heavy. I wondered if he had been weeping, but dismissed the notion. The idea of a man crying was ridiculous.

Mr. Lock seemed surprised to see me on the landing, and he looked at me with a little suspicion. He knew Mrs. Cotton's rotas as well as she knew his. I shouldn't really have been there.

"Miss Tamper, can I help you?"

I asked if I could trouble him for the key to the storeroom, as I needed more blacking for the grates.

"Couldn't this have waited?" Mr. Lock asked irritably.

"Sorry, sir," I said, "but Mrs. Cotton—"

"It's quite all right, Mr. Lock," interrupted His Lordship. "I am aware that my sister-in-law runs a tight ship. Better see to the young girl's problems. I believe our conversation was concluded."

Mr. Lock bowed shallowly and I followed him down the stairs, thinking about what they'd been discussing. After seeing my mother pass away under this roof, the idea of watching Samuel do the same wrenched at my heart. I made a promise then that I would do everything in my power to make him comfortable and help him recover.

In the kitchen, Mr. Lock opened the storeroom and stepped aside.

"Go on, then," he said. "Fetch what you need."

I thought for a moment that he might watch me, but he stepped back from the narrow doorway. The storeroom had shelves on either side, filled with spare napkins and cloths, brushes and pans.

At the far end were the cleaning products: the powders and liquids for making the various polishes, ointments and cleaning fluids that were needed in the house. Such things could be bought ready-made, but we used to joke that Mrs. Cotton preferred to spend the housekeeping money on herself. One of Lizzy's most hated jobs was the mixing of ingredients—something I was happy not to be trusted with.

It struck me that there were things in here that could poison a person: antimony for furniture polish, lead coating for the pipes, sealed flypaper that smelled rancid when left out—what was that covered with? Some sort of toxic chemical, surely. There were other sealed pots with names I couldn't pronounce. There were bottle of acids too, with dust-covered labels.

But I couldn't linger. On top of a small chest was a pile of writing pads. I took a single sheet and a new pencil, tucking them into my apron pouch. Then I bent down to fetch the blacking.

I must have been blushing as I came out, but Mr. Lock didn't notice. He was sitting at the bottom of the main stairs, his hands resting on his knees. His skin had taken on a curious grey color, and when he looked up at me, his watery blue eyes were unfocused.

"Is everything all right, sir?" I asked.

He nodded briskly, then rose stiffly, locked the door to the store and walked slowly away. At the foot of the stairs he paused, and put up a hand to steady himself against the frame.

"It's been a year since your mother went, hasn't it, Abi?"

Odd, I thought, because he never used my Christian name.

"It has, sir," I replied.

Mr. Lock's shoulders seemed to sag a little. "Time passes quickly, does it not?"

I wasn't sure what he meant, but I said it did.

He took the stairs slowly, as though carrying a great burden.

❈

I could hear Lizzy in her room, but she didn't come through to mine. I was grateful, both on account of our falling out and because I needed peace to write the letter to Dr. Reinhardt. I sat over the blank page, wondering how to begin. What could he actually tell me?

My worst fear was that he'd dismiss me immediately without a thought, so I took care to make my letters neat, and to sound as much like a grown-up as possible.

Dear Dr. Reinhardt,

I would very much like to engage your services on a delicate matter. My mother died some twelve months ago. It is my sincere belief that her spirit has not properly been laid to rest. Perhaps you could advise in a reply how we might seek to rectify this situation. You will understand that I wish to keep this matter private.

Yours sincerely,

Miss Abigail Tamper

I read it back, asking myself what he'd make of such a strange note. There seemed no other option. Either my mother's ghost was roaming the rooms of Greave Hall or I was losing my mind.

I folded the paper, and using a lighted candle, dripped wax over the fold. It pooled and hardened, sealing the letter. I wrote Dr. Reinhardt's name and address on the front, but gave no return address.

That was because I had other plans.

Fourteen

THE KITCHEN WAS STILL WARM FROM THE RANGE as we ate our dinner, which on a Sunday was always better than other days: skins from the potatoes roasted in leftover fat, cuts of meat from Lord Greave and Mrs. Cotton's joint, cabbage and sprouts stewed with cloves. The table was silent as we gorged. Every so often the bell would ring and Mr. Lock would go up to tend to the diners' needs.

Lizzy had not spoken more than a few words to me since our argument, but below stairs such animosity couldn't survive for long. Resentments couldn't be brushed beneath the carpet—they must either be addressed or allowed to fizzle out.

I asked her how her sister was, for that was where she had been until the evening.

"She's well," said Lizzy. "The baby's good as gold."

There was a rustle in the wall.

"Bloody mice," said Cook. "The sooner Rowena's up and running, the better."

"Them's not mice," said Rob. "I saw a rat the other day. Big as my foot, he was."

"Well then," said Cook. "Get some poison down, lad. There's some in the cellar, I think."

Greave Hall had been erected over the remains of another building, so my mother said, and there was another room below the kitchen and the scullery. It was enclosed within the foundations and lined by timber beams, with sagging walls. It was just a box, really, with no lights, and barely five feet high. The wine was kept down there, together with ice if we had any—and, as I now discovered, rat poison. I hadn't known about that till now.

Rob stood up from the table and went over to the hatch. It was opened by an old iron ring that was set into the floor. He looped a finger into the ring and gave a sharp tug. The hatch opened, bringing up a blast of damp air.

"Pass me a light, will you, Abi?"

I lit a candle with a spill from the fire in the range and carried it over.

I didn't like to go down in the cellar at all, and thankfully there was seldom need to. When I was just seven, I'd hidden beneath the hatch in a game of hide-and-seek with Samuel, and had somehow become trapped. It took him over an hour to find me, and all that time I was in the pitch darkness, feeling the cobwebs tickle my face.

From above I saw Rob searching. I made out a pile of rope, some broken furniture and some old pans. There were a couple of lengths of piping too, though they looked rusted in the orange light and good for nothing.

After some rummaging, Rob came up with a tin. He handed it to me together with the candle while he climbed back up the stepladder. Then he closed the hatch again, dusted himself down and returned to the table, placing the tin beside him.

"Mind you don't get that mixed up with the suet, Miss McMahon," he said.

Cook's eyes flashed. "And what would you be meaning by that?" she said.

Rob, who had been laughing, stopped. "Nothing, ma'am, of course. It was just a little jest, is all."

"Well, kindly keep such humor to yourself," she said.

An uncomfortable silence settled over the table, with the only sound the scraping of cutlery and Mr. Lock's toothless slurping on his soup.

My mother had barely eaten anything after she fell ill, and what she had consumed seemed to pass straight through her racked body or be vomited up again. But Cook had prepared it all, and, of course, everything she had eaten before her illness.

I shot a sideways glance at the great, red-faced woman. She was sucking the marrow from a bone. Her lips glistened and her eyes were screwed shut.

Soon after, Rob stood up. "Well, I must be seeing to Lancelot's feed," he said.

Cook grunted something and began to collect up the plates.

I was left to wash the pans and dinner plates while Cook cleaned the hearth. In the reflection of a copper pot, I saw her reach inside her apron and sneak a sip from her bottle. We all knew she drank, of course, and that much of her wages went on the worst sort of gin, but none of us pried. I think even Mrs. Cotton must have known.

Mr. Lock came in to collect the last of the china and lock it in the closet, safe for the night. "Will they be wanting coffee?" Cook asked.

"Just for Mrs. Cotton," said Mr. Lock. "His Lordship has retired for the night."

"Abi," said Cook, "make the coffee, would you, and take it in."

I did as I was asked, taking water from the range and pouring it over the ground beans. The rich and bitter smell wafted to my nostrils. I placed the filter in the pot and set it on a tray along with a jug of milk and bowl of sugar.

The rat poison, I noticed, was still on the table. What would happen, I wondered, if I put a little of it in the steaming pot? Cook was in the scullery and wouldn't know. The coffee would surely mask the taste.

The bell rang from the drawing room, shaking me from my idle thoughts. That's quite enough of that, I told myself.

I carried the tray quickly upstairs. The house was quiet now, and the windows were all dark. The clock chimed nine. I was looking forward to sinking into bed.

I balanced the tray on one hand and knocked on the drawing-room door. Mrs. Cotton's voice bade me enter. She was sitting at one end of a chaise lounge, wearing a blue dress with a navy cardigan over the top. Around her neck was a string of pearls, which presumably had once belonged to her sister. I set down the tray in front of her.

"Would you like me to pour?" I asked.

"And risk spilling on the carpet?" said Mrs. Cotton. "I think not."

"Will there be anything else, ma'am?"

"Yes, there will," she said. "I asked you to clean the windows earlier, did I not?"

"Yes, ma'am," I said. "I did them all."

"You're lying to my face, girl," she said. "The windows in Master Greave's room have not been cleaned. In fact, it looks as though you've been pawing them with your filthy little hands."

I didn't understand what she was saying. I'd made sure all the glass was spotless, especially that in the library.

"I shall look now, ma'am," I said, turning to leave.

"Wait!" said Mrs. Cotton. "Let me see your hands."

I held them out, turning them slowly so the housekeeper could see both sides. I had just been washing in the sink, so they were red raw but spotless. She shot out a hand and gripped my wrist.

At first I thought she just wanted to look more closely. She pulled my hand down towards her so that I had to bend down as well. Only when I came near the coffee pot did I realize this was something else.

I tried to pull away, but she held me fast. She was

so much stronger than she looked. All the time her fierce eyes held mine. I thought about calling for help, but who would have come? Mrs. Cotton made the rules, not me.

When my hand was an inch from the burning pot, she stopped.

"You hate me, don't you, Miss Tamper?" she whispered.

It was as if she could see into my heart and knew what I had considered doing in the kitchen.

"Answer me," she said. "Do you wish me dead?"

Tears welled in my eyes, not from the anticipated pain so much as the humiliation that she could cause them so easily.

"I do," I said.

At that, she smiled and released me. "At least you are sometimes honest," she said. "Now get out of my sight."

I rushed from the room.

Behind the door, I was breathing heavily. Mr. Lock passed me, carrying a tray of his own. On it were Lord

Greave's crystal decanter filled with cognac, and a single glass. It rattled as the old butler ascended the main staircase. It was one of the many rituals of the house—His Lordship's drink before bed. In times gone by Sammy had taken it to him, but now it was left to the old butler.

I went into the library and lit a lamp. I couldn't understand what Mrs. Cotton had said about the window, but as I held the light up to the glass I saw that it was true. Not just one print, but perhaps a dozen were spread across the pane—too many to have been caused by any accident. I fetched a cloth from the downstairs cupboard, wondering who might have done such a thing. Perhaps Lizzy, in anger at our cross words over Henry.

I set to wiping. The marks came off easily, but I was troubled. It seemed so trivial, so petty—not like Lizzy at all. As for Mrs. Cotton, she could have dreamt up a thousand worse privations to torment me. There was one print that wouldn't come off: a full hand, stretched out as if it had been pressed against the glass. I wiped over it twice, but it didn't even smear. I spat on the cloth and tried again. Still it remained.

My heart quickened as I realized why. It was on the outside.

I stepped back from the window, staring into the

blackness of the garden beyond. It had not been there earlier, I was sure, but somehow someone had left their mark on both the inside and the outside. The window was locked.

I crept forward slowly, and put my nose to the window pane. The garden was still, the plants and trees waving softly in a light breeze. The sash would only go up so far, and from the position of the print in the upper pane, I realized it would have had to be someone in the garden.

Out of curiosity, I placed my own right hand against the mark, so my fingertips met the contact points on the glass. Whoever had done this had hands slightly larger than my own.

I went down to the kitchen, and told Cook that I'd be going out to wipe away a mark on the library window. She was sitting in a chair beside the dying hearth with a ball of wool on her lap, the needles clicking against each other as she knitted.

"Don't be long," she said, smiling. "One search party a week is quite enough for me."

Mr. Lock hadn't yet secured the back door. The air was cold and dry, the sky clear but for a few shreds of cloud that swathed a full moon. I shivered, hurrying into the rear garden. The candle still burned in its stand where I'd left it in the room, casting thick shadows up the walls. Even stretching, I could not reach the mark, so I found an upturned vegetable crate in the stable yard and brought it round.

I stood precariously on top of the crate and raised the cloth. But something was wrong. I looked first at my own hand, then back at the mark.

The handprint had changed.

What had been a left hand pressed up to the glass was now the mark of a right hand. Doubting my own sanity, I again placed my right hand against the glass to check. There was no questioning it. Fear tickled along the back of my neck, lifting the hairs there. I rubbed the mark away, climbed quickly down from the crate and peered into the garden.

"Is anyone there?" I said.

Silence. The only light came from the clouded moon and the dim glow from the candle in the room behind. I could make out the tall rear garden wall and the trees, the clumps of bushes, the path running like a black river through the center of it all.

"Hello?" I said, louder this time.

"Robert Willmett!" I said, trying to sound scornful. "If this is your idea of another joke, then Cook is right and your sense of humor is sorely lacking."

The only answer I got was the faint rustle of leaves above.

A deeper darkness fell across my shoulders as though someone had moved close behind me. I spun round.

The candle in the library had gone out.

I couldn't help a yelp of fear and edged quickly along the back wall of the house towards the door. I kept my eyes strained against the gloom of the garden, certain that someone, or something, was there. With a shaking hand I found the door handle and pushed it down, then fell back inside, tripping over a bucket with a great clatter.

"Was on earth is it, child?" said Cook. She sat where I'd left her, knitting in her chair.

"Did anyone else go out there?" I asked.

"Why would they?" she replied. "It could chill the cloven feet of Satan himself if that draft is anything to go by."

I took her hint and closed the door, turning the key in the lock.

Fifteen

THE FOLLOWING MORNING THE HOUSE WAS ABUZZ with anticipation. Samuel was expected before noon, and Lord Greave came down dressed in his finest clothes. According to Mr. Lock, he was pacing the main rooms, checking that all the living arrangements were in order for the return of his son.

It was not until after ten, when I had emptied the pots and cleaned the first-floor water closet, that I heard the clop of hooves. My first thought was that Samuel was back earlier than expected, but a glance through the front window told me it was Adam. Monday was when he came by to pick up the grocery orders for the rest of the week, but there was something else I needed him for. I ran down the back steps.

Cook was handing over a list when I got there, saying that last time the potatoes had been mealy, so

Adam's face brightened when he saw me. He was a little cleaner today. I followed him back out to his cart, empty but for a few open crates, and gave Archer a stroke on the nose.

"I need you to do me a favor," I said.

"Oh, yes, ma'am," he said. "And what might that be?"

I looked back at the house to make sure no eyes were on us, then pulled out my letter to Dr. Reinhardt. "I need you to deliver this, but I have no money."

Adam took the letter in his grubby hand and studied it closely. I knew he could read a little, but I couldn't afford for this to go wrong.

"It's for a Dr. Reinhardt, 11b Argyle Terrace," I said. "Do you know it?"

"I do," he said. "'Bout a mile from here." He looked at me, puzzled, but I remained silent.

"Well?" he said. "You going to tell me any more?"

"Not now," I said. "Will you do it for me?"

"What's in it for yours truly?" he said. "I'll be traipsing halfway across London."

I let my shoulders sag. "I don't have anything. Not now. Maybe later."

Adam folded his skinny arms and made a show of looking unimpressed. "I'll do it for a kiss," he said.

"What?"

"You heard," he said. He turned his cheek to the side and pointed to a spot. "A kiss, right there, and I'll take your letter."

I checked back to the house again, then leaned forward. He had closed his eyes, I noticed. I chose the least dirty spot I could see, and planted a peck on his cheek.

He opened his eyes, blushing.

"And can you wait for a reply, please?" I asked him. "I don't want anyone here knowing I've sent a letter."

Adam tut-tutted and turned to Archer. "It's a good thing all our customers aren't so demanding, ain't it, fella?" he said.

I thanked him again, and watched the cart trundle off down the road. I'd put all my hopes in that young boy and Dr. Reinhardt. I prayed they wouldn't let me down.

Before I went back indoors, I hurried to the stables to check on Rowena. Sure enough, three kittens were snuggled up by her belly, suckling with their eyes closed. Another, I noticed, lay still in a corner. Three out of four alive wasn't bad, but with Adam already on his way, I wasn't sure what to do with them. I went across the stable to get another handful of straw, and placed it carefully around them, then I crouched beside Rowena and gave her a stroke. The little ones cheeped blindly like baby birds.

"Clever girl," I whispered. "I'll come back later."

By noon, there was still no sign of Samuel. Two visitors arrived first, and their presence sent the staff below stairs into a spell of wretched anxiety. Dr. Ingle was admitted with his satchel. He brought another man with him who, we were told, was his son David, in training to take over the practice after his father retired. David Ingle was a fresh-faced young man of twenty-two, with a nervous, fidgeting air and short sandy hair. They talked for some time with Lord Greave in the drawing room and inspected the library where Samuel would be staying. Dr. Ingle Senior departed shortly afterwards, leaving his son with His Lordship.

Duties were forgotten in the tense hour that followed. Lord Greave and David ate a hasty lunch of bread, cheese and jellied fruit, which Mr. Lock took up to the sitting room. At just after one, the doorbell rang.

We all looked at each other nervously as Mrs. Cotton went upstairs.

A few minutes later, the housekeeper summoned us all. We were to line up in the front hallway to welcome back her nephew. Cook smoothed the wiry springs of her hair back under her shawl and Lizzy and I stood close beside her. Across the hall stood Rob, straight as a rod. He opened the door as hoofbeats sounded in the road.

A carriage with military insignia waited outside, and Lord Greave and Mr. Lock shared hurried words with the driver. We saw His Lordship peer through the carriage's window and his body stiffen. He called for Rob.

Lizzy gave my hand a squeeze.

The driver opened the carriage door. I knew it was improper to look, but I glanced quickly from the corner of my eye. Rob reached into the interior, and when he emerged, an arm was draped over his shoulders. With some difficulty, he and the driver hoisted Samuel Greave from the carriage.

I quickly turned back to face front, but in my brief glance I'd seen enough. Samuel was in his uniform—the blue pantaloons and gold braiding of the 13th Light Dragoons. I had not studied his face in any detail, but I saw he still had the dashing moustache, grown in a hurry once his orders had come through. His right leg was heavily bandaged from knee to ankle and his foot was bare.

He was helped up the front step, leaning heavily on

the footman and the driver.

"This way, sir," said Rob.

I caught a peek at his face again as he was supported through the door and towards the library. There was a sheen of sweat across his pale skin, and his lips were drawn back across his teeth in a grimace of pain. The bandages on his leg looked clean enough, but with him came a smell that reminded me of meat which has turned in the heat. He hardly seemed to see me as he passed by.

While Samuel was made at home in his new room, Rob fetched in three cases from the carriage as well as two crutches. He deposited them in the library then left, closing the door behind him. Lord Greave, Mrs. Cotton, Mr. Lock and David Ingle remained inside with Samuel. Muffled cries came through the door and seemed to echo up the stairs, filling the house. He had been suppressing his agonies for our sake.

"Poor lad," said Cook. "Poor, brave boy."

I suppose she too was remembering the Samuel of a year before, returning from the stores freshly kitted out. He had strode down the back steps and into the scullery to show us his new uniform, his face flushed with pride, his hand on the tasselled hilt of a glistening sabre.

I had been too eager with anticipation, then numbed with shock, to feel much, but seeing the tears in Cook's eyes made my own prick—for Samuel certainly, but for my mother too. For she had been in the scullery that day, alive and well, and had said how handsome young Samuel looked.

Mrs. Cotton came from the room shortly after, her face unreadable.

We quickly dispersed. I had to clean away the plates from His Lordship's luncheon in the sitting room—a room I hadn't entered since the fearful night of Dr. Reinhardt's visit. Now, with the furniture righted, the fire blazing in the hearth and the sepia light of the afternoon sun coming through the windows, it was hard to believe what I had witnessed in there.

I could do nothing until I spoke to the doctor again, and diverted my attention by going to Rowena. When I was sure Mrs. Cotton was back in her bedroom, I ran out to the stables. The three little kittens squeaked in panic as I placed them one by one in my apron. Rowena seemed to know I was there to help. She let me pick her up and carry her back indoors. I kissed her on the neck and whispered, "You'll be warm again soon."

There was only one place I could think to take her, and that was the spare bedroom at the back of the house. No one ever went in there, as far as I could tell, so the new mother was unlikely to be disturbed.

Once she was installed behind an old wardrobe, I soaked some bread in milk for her, and took it up. She ate hungrily and purred in contentment. The kittens latched on again quickly and resumed their single-minded sucking.

Sixteen

FOR THE NEXT TWO DAYS, THE HOUSE WENT through its routines. Sammy was confined to the library, attended only by Mr. Lock, Mrs. Cotton and His Lordship. He ate nothing but soup, and little enough of that, according to Cook. Lord Greave took his meals in his room and seemed to shrink back into himself again. He stopped dressing himself properly and took to wandering aimlessly around the rear garden, sucking on his pipe and mumbling under his breath.

Dr. Ingle's son called twice each day, to change the bandages on Samuel's legs and check that the patient was otherwise all right. It was late on Wednesday afternoon when he came running down from the library and asked Rob to summon his father and a surgeon quickly.

Dr. Ingle Senior arrived shortly after with a broad-shouldered, bald-headed man whose stomach burgeoned beneath a waistcoat and whose sleeves were already rolled up. I felt sure then that Samuel was near the end. He was making no sound at all that we could hear.

There was no way I could know what was about to happen on the other side of the door, but the feeling that settled over the house was like the heavy air before a storm breaks, when everyone waits for the first huge crack of thunder that will split the heavens open.

We all stopped our work and felt the rooms vibrate with an almost painful anticipation. Then came the awful sounds from the library. A strangled wail, as though His Lordship's son was facing his worst fear and trying to push it away. Animal groans, and then above them a rhythmic whine—back and forth, back and forth. Others were grunting too and the surgeon was shouting, "Hold him steady! It's over soon."

Lizzy was crying, as was I. Cook looked away to stop us seeing her tears. We all knew, I think, what was happening in that room, but the image of it was too awful to contemplate: a saw's blade working its way through flesh and bone.

Mr. Lock came down to the scullery and his face was grey and tinged with yellow. The front of his shirt was flecked with blood, his cuffs soaked red.

"Water," he said. "Hot water."

We rushed to fill a pail. "Shall I carry it?" I asked.

He took it from me without a word and retreated upstairs. As he opened the door again, all we could hear was Sammy's frail voice moaning "Oh! oh!" to no one but himself.

The surgeon was shown out first at about five o'clock. His tread was as steady as when he had arrived, but when I came to think of it later, I realised that he was carrying an extra burden in that bag of brutal tools—everything below Samuel Greave's right knee.

We all understood it was touch and go for Samuel after the operation and we trod carefully outside the library door so as not to disturb him. It was hard to ignore his pain though. Often he would cry out when his bandages were changed, and we had the daily reminders of his suffering in the gauze and linens we had to wash. Lord Greave didn't leave his room.

To be honest, I was now dreading seeing Sammy again. Would he really have time for a little girl who knew nothing of war and wounds and had never even traveled over the Thames, let alone the Black Sea?

As it was, the choice wasn't mine.

"Miss Tamper," said Mrs. Cotton two days after the surgeon had visited, "come at once to the library and bring cold water and a towel."

I filled a large bowl, draped a towel over my arm and followed Mrs. Cotton up the stairs. I dreaded what I might see on entering the room, but promised myself that I would do my duty without flinching.

Young Dr. Ingle stood outside the library door. The bowl was beginning to weigh heavy in my arms.

"This is the girl?" he said.

"It is," said Mrs. Cotton. "Miss Tamper has been with us for many years and knows Master Greave well."

"Very good," he said. The doctor stooped to face me. "Miss Tamper, His Lordship's son is very sick indeed. The exertion of his voyage back to England, then the operation—he has a dire fever."

I forgot about the heavy bowl. What was he telling me—that Samuel was going to die? It seemed so unjust after the pain he had fought through already.

"Will he be all right?" I said.

Mrs. Cotton sniffed as if I should have kept my mouth shut, but the doctor pursed his lips in a sympathetic smile. "It is in God's hands now, whether or not he lives."

"You are to be excused your normal duties for the rest of the day," said Mrs. Cotton sharply. "Stay with Master Samuel and do not leave his side."

"He will require frequent fluids, either water or ale,"

said the doctor. "Make sure he is comfortable—that is
the main thing. And if his condition deteriorates further,
send young Willmett for me immediately. Do you
understand?"

"I do, sir," I said.

He nodded firmly. "Good."

Mrs. Cotton opened the door, and in I went.

Dr. Ingle Senior sat beside the bed. He was leaning
over Samuel and replacing a small glass bottle in his
satchel, which he then closed before straightening up.
Lord Greave stood facing the window, looking out onto
the lawns. The room smelled stale and lived-in, a little
like Lancelot's stables. Samuel lay back with the sheets
pulled up to his throat. The lines of his lower body were
visible beneath the bedclothes, the left leg extending
beyond the right. His head was rolled to one side on the
pillows and his eyes half open, still as a millpond. My
first horrible thought was that he had died, but I saw the
quilt was rising and falling slowly with his weak breath.

I placed the bowl of water on the table near the
head of the bed and gave a curtsy. Dr. Ingle's eyes
lingered on me for a second, and I saw the fleeting
remembrance of the night of my attempted escape. "I'll
leave you now, sir," he said.

Lord Greave turned and nodded. His face was

drawn, painted with weariness and grief. "Thank you, Donald," he said. "I'll see you out."

They left me in there, alone with Samuel. I dabbed the towel in the water and leaned over the pillows. His dark hair was slick across his temples. From a foot away, I could feel the heat that came off his body like a furnace. I brushed the hair away and dabbed at his forehead with the cloth. His eyelids flickered and opened a fraction. His dark pupils rolled back to focus on me. Even in his weakness, his look seemed to hold so many emotions in conflict with one another. Confusion. Recognition. Maybe even fear. His lips moved and he breathed my name.

"Abi . . ."

"I'm here," I said. "Sammy."

"So hot," he said.

I leaned across him to fold back the bedclothes a little. His chest was bare, the muscles taut and hairless. His breastbone protruded beneath his pale skin.

"You're home, now, Sammy," I said, laying the cool cloth over his head.

"Home," he said. "Yes."

His eyes drifted closed, as though the word itself had acted as a salve to his pain.

Seventeen

THROUGH THAT WEEKEND, SAMUEL DRIFTED IN and out of fevered consciousness and I barely left his side other than to fetch more water, or coal to keep the fire blazing. I felt sorry for Lizzy, for she had to carry out the tasks that would have otherwise fallen to me.

It was not hard work, but it was tiring nonetheless. I found myself attuned to Samuel's suffering, almost as if it were my own. Each groan or sigh, each shift beneath the sheets, each time his face contorted with pain or an awful dream I would lean forward, whispering words of encouragement or offering a sip of water. At night I slept fitfully in a chair pulled up beside the bed, waking stiffly before dawn.

Those two days blurred together into one specific incident that I can never forget, even though I might want to. Samuel had been sleeping at peace for most of the morning and I was in danger of dropping off myself. The room was warmed through, and the air seemed to press down on me. I stood to get the blood flowing once again to my legs. I passed the shelves and my eye caught the spine of my favorite book—*Ivanhoe*. It had been four years at least since I had last read it.

The books were locked behind a door, but the key was in the lock. The covering was more to protect the volumes from dust and decay than for security. I doubted that Lord Greave or Sammy would care if I took it out to pass the hours. It could hardly be counted a dereliction of duty, as long as I stayed at Samuel's side. Mrs. Cotton was another matter. The only thing I'd ever seen her read was a Bible, and if she came into the room, I might not have time to hide the book. But she hadn't bothered me at all for the past few days. I had passed her two or three times below stairs, and she had offered no comment other than the disapproval in her pursed lips.

Nor had she inquired as to the welfare of her nephew. I think she was pleased to be rid of the responsibility. It struck me then that it was perhaps she who had instigated this arrangement. I had wondered why I, perhaps the least suitable candidate, had been chosen to nurse Samuel. Was it because the housekeeper thought I was most likely to fail, that His Lordship's son would perish in my care? It seemed the most likely explanation. What would happen to me then? I wondered. Might it even be deemed that I was to blame?

Such thoughts gave me renewed determination. I had not been able to save my mother, but Samuel would be different.

I turned the key in the lock and took out the leather-bound copy, then resumed my position beside the invalid silently. It wasn't long before I was engrossed in the pages. I read avidly for upwards of two hours, drinking in the words like a person parched with thirst. When the clock struck two it was a surprise how quickly time had passed. At that time Samuel was managing only two meals a day, if a few sips of soup can be called a meal, and it was clear that he was losing weight. The bones of his face, especially around his eye sockets, seemed to protrude more by the hour.

I closed the book and placed it beneath the head of his bed, then left the room. Cook warmed through some of the weak broth of beef and vegetables, which I carried back upstairs.

Outside the library door, something made me pause. I cannot say quite why. Perhaps it was fear. I felt sure that someone was inside—someone besides Samuel.

The feeling passed and I told myself to get a grip of my emotions. Balancing the tray on one hand, I pushed open the door.

The room was the same, the fire blazing and Samuel lying there with the sheets pulled up to his neck. The windows were steamed up so that it was impossible to see very much outside. The single lamp burned beside the bed.

But there was a different smell—a smell of burning, and more than just the sooty aroma of combusting coal. I wondered for a moment if a spark had jumped the fireguard. I scanned the carpet in front of the fire. There was nothing.

I placed the tray of broth and bread on the small bedside table. Samuel's eyelids flickered open, and he turned his head weakly towards me.

"You must eat something," I said.

He seemed too weak even to smile, but gave a tiny nod.

I laid a napkin across the sheet by his chin, then ran a hand beneath his pillow and tried to lift his neck a fraction. He responded, the cords in his neck straining, and opened his lips for the spoon. I tipped the broth in and saw his Adam's apple bob as he swallowed. We managed half a dozen more mouthfuls before he sank back again. The effort had pushed a fresh sheen of sweat on his pale skin. Within seconds he was asleep once more.

I put the bowl aside, deciding that I wouldn't remove it just yet, in case he recovered the strength to eat more.

I reached down to get my book.

I reached farther beneath the bed.

I got down on my hands and knees and peered along the floor.

The book had gone.

The room suddenly felt hotter still, the only sound the crackling of the fire. Before I even looked, I knew what I would see. I stood slowly and walked to the fire. In the grate, on top of the coals, were the charred remains of Sir Walter Scott's *Ivanhoe*.

A faint threatened to overcome me and I had to steady myself against the mantelpiece. I looked again into the hearth. Surely my mind was playing tricks on me? But no. It was there, and there could be no denying the evidence before my eyes. The pages of the book had all but gone, and the leather binding glowed red. Flakes of ash were drifting up the chimney.

I looked at Samuel, lying asleep. A dozen thoughts were fighting for ascendance in my brain. He couldn't possibly reach beneath the bed in his condition—a man who could barely take a mouthful of soup from a spoon. And even if he could, how would he walk across the room with only a single leg to stand on?

With my back to the door, and fear gripping me, a word came to my lips before I could stop it.

"Mother?" I whispered.

There was no answer. Samuel's low breathing was regular. The fire crackled softly.

Eighteen

UNDER THE PRETEXT OF FILLING THE LAMP WITH fresh oil, I went back to the scullery. For safety, we kept the oil outside in a storeroom adjacent to the stable block. Rob was out there mixing something in a bucket, his sleeves rolled up to his elbows.

"You all right, m'lady?" he said. "White as a freshly laundered sheet."

"Just a little chill," I said. "It's devilish cold out here."

"That it is," he said. "Old Lancelot's got a rheumy chest too." He nodded towards the stable, where the horse normally poked out his long nose.

"Will he be better soon?" I asked.

"Soon as he gets some of this inside, he will," said Rob. "He's not so used to all this exercise no more."

As I filled the lamp in the storeroom door, Rob carried the bucket into the stall. He handed me a bottle.

"Put this back on the shelf in there, would you?"

The label on the bottle showed a horse in a field, and above it the words "Newnham's Finest Equine Tonic." Beneath, it said: "Danger, not for human consumption."

I put the bottle on the shelf, feeling an odd sense of unease.

Rob was latching the stable door as I came out with the full lamp. I had thought him the only person quick enough to place fingerprints on the window or agile enough to snatch at my hand three stories up.

As I passed him, my eyes welled up with frustration. I was the lowliest person in the house. How could I hope to find a murderer in our midst? And what could I do without evidence, without proof? If my mother's spirit, or ghost, wanted to speak to me, why not find some means other than the frightening encounters so far? It was as though she was angry.

And then it struck me: she *was* angry. What had Dr. Reinhardt said? That it wasn't safe for me here. That I should leave. But I had not listened. I had stayed and tried to find out more, but perhaps that wasn't what my mother wanted at all. She wanted to thrust me out of

Greave Hall and away from danger.

I walked back up the stairs to the library, and my fear evaporated.

"I'm not going anywhere," I said to myself and to whoever else might be listening.

Like a storm that rages overnight, leaving a clear bright morning, by the following day Samuel's fever seemed to have lifted. The dark hours had passed undisturbed.

I had shuffled the books on the shelves so that *Ivanhoe* would not be found missing unless anyone took particular care to check.

Samuel's eyes were bright when I awoke, and they were focused on me.

"Good morning, Abigail," he said. His voice was dry as old leaves.

"Sammy!" I said.

"I'm too old for that now," he replied. "Call me Master Greave."

"I'm sorry, sir," I said quickly.

A slow smile crept over his cracked lips. "I'm joking, Abi."

I laughed, and he did too, until it turned into a coughing fit. I offered him water and he managed to push himself up in the bed and take the cup himself. He drank deeply for the first time in days. "I had an awful nightmare," he said. "A man was holding me down while another was taking off my leg . . ."

I couldn't look at him as he spoke, and lowered my eyes. "Samuel . . . "

". . . but now I see that it was no dream," he continued, with a heavy sigh. "I suppose it's better to be here four-fifths a man than no man at all."

I found the courage to look at him again.

"That's right," I said, then felt stupid. *What do I know?*

"Nelson only had one arm, and it did him no harm."

He took another drink, draining the cup once more, then he spoke of the long journey home by cart, steamer and train. He remembered only fragments through the pain—they had given him morphine whenever they could. One of his clearest recollections, he said, was the ship's doctor declaring it a certainty that he would keep his leg. He went silent then.

"They told us you were very brave," I said, "when it happened."

He blushed. He'd always done so as a child, and I was glad to see that hadn't changed.

"No braver than every other man," he replied. "It was dawn. We were in a charge, towards a fortified position of Russian guns along a low pass. The Captain thought we'd be on 'em before they had time to find their range, but they're quick buggers – pardon my language—those artillery boys. We were barely into a gallop when the shrapnel started flying." He passed a hand over his face, as though trying to wipe away the memory.

"You don't have to tell me," I said.

"No," he said. "It's fine, really. No harm can come of it now." He swept a lock of hair from his forehead. "My horse must have taken a hit, because he went down underneath me, and I was on the ground. The rest of the cavalry were charging past, sabres out and howling, when I saw another mount. He was riderless, so I scrambled towards him. Next thing I know, there's a great thud, and that's that. I woke up later when they were stretchering me off. One of the others said a cannonball thundered straight past me. Must have caught me on the way."

"How awful!" I said. "You must have been in great pain."

"Not really," he said. "Not till later. The whole thing was a bloody disaster. I say, don't cry, Abi."

I hadn't realized that I was until he wiped my cheek with his thumb. It's hard to understand, but for a few moments at least I'd forgotten about my mother completely and I was in a battlefield in the Crimea, hearing the screams of men and dying horses, the pounding of the Russian cannon. It was a long way from *Ivanhoe*.

"I'm sorry," I said. "You're the one who's suffering."

"Nonsense," he said brightly. "Now, if you'll excuse me for a moment, there's something I must do." He pointed to the chamber pot on the other side of the bed.

Now it was my turn to blush. "Of course," I said, moving towards the door. "I'll let His Lordship know you are feeling a little better. Mrs. Cotton too."

"Oh," he said. "She's still lodging with us, is she?"

I nodded, trying not to give my own emotions away.

"I'm so glad you're back, Sammy."

Everyone in the house was delighted that Samuel had come through the worst of it. Everyone, that is, apart from Mrs. Cotton.

"You'll be able to pull your weight again then, Miss

Tamper," she said. "I'm afraid Elizabeth has hardly been able to pick up the slack in your absence."

Though Samuel didn't leave the library, the doctors came again and declared him on the road to good health. They suggested at least a week before he used his crutches. My duties resumed as they'd always been—a daily toil between six in the morning and nine at night.

It was a Wednesday when I saw Adam again. Cook had been called upon to prepare a celebratory banquet and had fallen into a fluster. With her checking all the supplies as they were carried through the door, I feared I wouldn't get a chance to speak to him alone. Then he handed Cook a sack of potatoes and as she struggled through the door, he pulled an envelope from his pocket.

"There you are, me darlin'," he said.

On the envelope, in the finest copperplate writing, was the name Miss A. Tamper. I slipped it into my dress pouch, gave him a wink, and hurried back inside.

Later, when I was brushing the carpets on the stairs, I reached for the envelope, all the time alert for the faintest sound of footsteps.

My fingers were shaking as I opened it. Inside was a single sheet, folded once.

Dear Miss Abigail,

I read your note with interest, and sincerely believe that my skills might be of service to you. I understand, of course, the need for discretion in such delicate matters, and would therefore suggest that we meet for a private consultation. Please either provide your return address, or come by at my rooms. I am at home on Sundays from four o'clock, and Thursday's from six.

Your faithful servant,
Dr. M. Reinhardt

I read and reread the letter until its details were fixed in my memory, then burned it in the kitchen fire when Cook wasn't looking. If my mother could—or would—not speak to me directly, here was a man who had the ability to help.

But there was no way I could invite the doctor to Greave Hall. I had to go and see him. If Mrs. Cotton discovered me again, it would mean a beating at the very least. But there was a difference now: Samuel was home, and he held more sway than the housekeeper.

And this time I wasn't running away. This time I would be coming back.

Nineteen

I STRUGGLED TO SLEEP THAT NIGHT. I wound the watch and lay on my back, looking at the ceiling, and my high hopes sank like a soggy pudding. The following day was a Thursday, a day the doctor had said he would be at home, but the more I dwelled on it, the more unfeasible it seemed. How could I possibly get away? There'd be more chance of escaping from Millbank Jail.

As it was, an unexpected chance came my way.

A sound of retching woke me before dawn. My first thought was that Samuel had been taken ill again in the night, but the noise was closer than that. It came from across the hall. I crept out of bed and knocked on Elizabeth's door.

"Lizzy?"

"Abi?"

I went in and found her kneeling on the floor, with

one hand resting on the bedpost and another steadying her pot. Her skin was pale and sweating.

"Are you all right?" I said.

Her answer was another heave of her stomach. "It's nothing," she said. "Please, leave me be."

Her words were harsh, but I could see they stemmed from embarrassment rather than anger, and so I left. Still, her condition gave me cause for unease. I had known Lizzy for three years, and never once had she fallen ill. We all shared the same meals below stairs, and although I was tired, my stomach was fine. Cook looked rosy too, though she always had a fine flush in her cheeks.

I took care of the fires and went about my other morning duties. The dining room was given special attention as we were receiving guests that evening— the Ambroses from across the Park. No more was said of Lizzy's illness and by noon, when we set about the task of preparation together, she seemed to have recovered. She busied herself with the silver and china while I polished the furniture. We brought out the best candlesticks and made sure the lamps were filled and the wicks trimmed, and took great care over setting the table to Mrs. Cotton's satisfaction.

We were told that there would be three guests—Lord Greave's old friends Malcolm and Esme Ambrose and their son Alexander, a chum of Samuel's. I'd come to know Alex well when I was younger and permitted to take part in some of their games, but it had been almost two years since I had seen him. I saw that Lizzy looked up anxiously when his name was mentioned. She, of course, was thinking of the footman Henry.

It came as a surprise, though, that with three guests, we were asked to set only five places at the great mahogany table. Cook said that Mrs. Cotton was dining out that evening at a friend's house, and so wouldn't be joining the others in the dining room at Greave Hall. It was Rob who said what we were all thinking.

"Strange night to be abandoning the rest of the family, isn't it? Big to-do like this?"

Cook, who was busy rolling pastry on the flour-dusted table, looked up.

"Well, it's not our business to pry now, is it?"

That shut Rob up, and he muttered about tidying up the yard, then left.

What he'd said was right though. By all accounts that night's feasting was to be a celebration of Samuel's convalescence, and Mrs. Cotton choosing not to join in struck me as rather odd too. However, it gave me an unexpected opportunity—I had more chance of getting out of the house and away to Dr. Reinhardt. But there were plenty of other obstacles: for a start, I was sure to be called upon to help at supper.

After lunch, the housekeeper left us all with strict instructions and retired to her room to prepare for her evening out. The guests were due to arrive at five o'clock, and there was still much to be done. I was walking past the library when I heard a muffled bang and curse within.

I opened the door without knocking. Samuel was leaning against a bookshelf, steadying himself. On the ground beside him lay his crutch. To my surprise he was already dressed for dinner, with a crisp white shirt and tie. He had shaved, but wore no jacket.

"Oh, Abi," he said. "Good. Help me, will you?"

I hurried forward and picked up the crutch, holding it for him while he adjusted his position and managed the maneuver it back beneath his armpit.

"Should you be up?" I said. "Perhaps we should wait for Rob to help."

"Nonsense," he said, breathing heavily. He was obviously in some pain. "I thought I'd take a little turn about the garden."

"Is that wise?"

"Probably not," he grimaced, "but perhaps you could join me if Mrs. Cotton can spare you."

I found Lock, who had a key to the French windows. He said he didn't think it was a good idea for the young master to be going out, but Samuel insisted. And so, in lurches and painful steps, with me hovering in case of an accident, we shambled outside.

As children, we had played together in the garden many times. One of my earliest memories was climbing into the branches of the plum tree at the far end and looking back towards the house. My mother had been in the nursery, standing at the window and looking on with her arms folded and a proud smile.

Now, with winter, all the colors were muted. Tears sprang up before I could prevent them.

"I shall be all right, you know," said Samuel.

I realized that he had got the wrong impression. He thought I was crying for him.

"Oh, it's not that," I said. "I was thinking of my mother."

His skin colored with embarrassment.

"Of course," he said. "How silly of me. You miss her badly?"

I missed her like an ache deep in my gut. Sadness climbed through my body like the tide sliding up a shallow beach, threatening to drown me.

"I do," I said simply.

Samuel put his arm around my shoulder and squeezed. "I do, too. She was like a mother to me. Certainly more so than my aunt."

Rules governed everything we did, everything we said. But Samuel could puncture it all in a second. It didn't matter that he was the master and I the servant. As we reached the end of the path and stood under the spindly boughs of the plum tree, I worked up courage to ask a question.

"Samuel," I said, "why is it, do you suppose, that Mrs. Cotton is not dining with you tonight?"

He smiled—first a puzzled twitch of his lip, then a broader grin that showed his teeth. "Why do you ask, Abi?"

It was my turn to blush. "I shouldn't have asked."

Silence descended over our little meeting, and a breeze shook the branches of the tree and made me shiver.

"I asked that she absent herself," he said finally. His tone was so frank, so open.

"Why?"

He ran his hands over the tree bark. "Do you remember when we used to climb this tree, Abi?"

"Of course," I said. "My mother always told me not to go too high, or else the branch would break and I would hurt myself."

"You didn't listen though."

"No," I said, "and it never broke."

I couldn't help thinking that our conversation meant something more than either of us said. That he was trying to say something to me that he dare not speak outright.

"It is my belief that my aunt takes liberties that she should not," he said quickly.

He looked as if he was going to go on, so I didn't say anything, but my heart was racing. I longed to speak more, to tell him about the strange and terrifying events of late. For here he was, opening a door to me, giving me an opportunity to share my doubts with him about Mrs. Cotton.

"Sammy . . ." I said.

A sudden shiver passed over my skin. No breeze had caused it, for the branches were still and the air was silent. I turned back towards the house, certain in that moment that I would see something there in the nursery window—see my mother, watching as she had watched while she was alive.

But there wasn't anyone there.

"Come," Sammy said. "You're cold. Let's go back inside."

Twenty

I SAW SAMUEL BACK TO THE LIBRARY, WHERE HE said he would take a nap before dinner, then went about my duties. I was still convinced that it would take some unlikely stroke of luck to allow me to leave the house that evening, and had largely put the idea from my mind.

With the dusting done and the coal scuttles refilled in every room, I went upstairs to change into my serving clothes. It was as I entered my own room that I heard a noise from Lizzy's. My first thought was that she was taken ill again, so I knocked.

There was no answer.

"Elizabeth?" I said, peering round the door.

The room was empty.

I paused with a foot on the threshold. I had tried to forget the events in the garden, but now the image of that handprint came to my mind. I crouched to look under her bed.

Only floorboards covered in dust.

Against the near wall in Lizzy's room stood an old wardrobe, worm-eaten and scratched. I steeled myself and strode into the room to look round the side.

"Found you!" I said.

There was no one there.

Then a soft knocking came from within the wardrobe itself, as though something were butting up against the door.

My mouth was dry, my hands clammy with sweat.

"Lizzy?" I said, in barely a whisper.

The gentle thudding stopped.

Even though I knew there must be a logical explanation—that either Rob or Lizzy must be inside—I still felt reluctant to look. My racing heart told me to leave the room at once, but my mind told me that I could not. I placed my hands on the worn doorknob and pulled.

Lizzy's clothes hung neatly within. Her shoes were lined up along the bottom, her undergarments stacked in a pile. Nothing moved. My breath burst forth in a rush.

But there, lying on top of Lizzy's folded polishing smock, was her scarf—the gift from Henry. It took me a moment to realize that something was wrong with the frayed edge. It had been torn in half.

I picked up the two pieces in bewilderment. Had something happened to cause Lizzy to do such a thing? They must have fallen out. Poor Lizzy! No wonder she had been acting so strangely.

"Abi?"

Lizzy's voice made me turn round. She was standing in the doorway, staring at me. Her eyes dropped to the scarf, and the blood seemed to drain from her face. She gave a tiny shake of her head then stepped forward. I saw her hand flash up and her palm whipcracked against my cheek. I staggered and steadied myself against the wardrobe door. My face felt as if it was being stabbed with a hundred tiny needle points. "How could you!" she shouted. "You heartless—"

"I—It wasn't me," I said. I shielded my face as she came closer. "I found it like that, I swear. I heard—"

"Get out!" said Lizzy, the tears already forming in her eyes. She snatched the scraps of material from my hand. "Get out," she sobbed.

I tried to explain further, but she was pushing me from the room. I fell out into the tiny corridor and heard her throw her weight against the other side of the door. After a few moments came the sound of quiet sobbing.

I went back to my room and as the mark of her palm faded on my cheek I wondered what was happening in the house. How could she think I would do such a terrible thing?

For an awful moment, I thought perhaps I was

responsible. Perhaps I had somehow washed the memory away, or replaced it with another. But no: I *was* in my right mind, I was sure of it.

A spirit must find its rest.

Dr. Reinhardt's words seemed to resonate now even more than they had done in his front parlor that day. But what had my mother's spirit got against poor Lizzy?

The afternoon that had begun with such an unpleasant scene got steadily worse. Not an hour after the altercation with Lizzy, there followed an uncomfortable reminder that even with Samuel home, things were not as they should be in Greave Hall.

I washed and changed into my serving clothes, making sure I was spick-and-span. I was used to serving at table, but rarely for guests. Whenever Mrs. Cotton entertained her ladies, it was Lizzy who was called upon rather than me. And tonight was special: I wanted to make a good impression for Samuel.

As I reached the top of the servants' stairs, there was a cry—Lord Greave's voice, raised in a high-pitched wail. I went down to the landing and saw a shoe bounce down the main stairs from his rooms, landing at my feet. I bent down to pick it up, and a second spun through the air and almost hit me.

"I told you," shouted Lord Greave, "I won't!"

"Come, sir," said Mr. Lock patiently. "Your guests will be here soon."

I fetched the second shoe from outside Mrs. Cotton's door. Both were polished to such a high shine that I could see my face in the toes.

"Damn my guests!" shouted His Lordship.

He pushed past Lock and appeared at the top of the steps. He was wearing only an undershirt and a pair of socks, and his white knees were sticking out. I looked away at once.

"Forgive me, sir," I said. "I was only—"

Then I was being bustled away by Mr. Lock, his face flushed.

"Is His Lordship all right?" I asked.

"Of course," he said in an exasperated tone. "Please, go about your business."

He returned upstairs as quickly as his creaking body would allow. I heard Lord Greave's laughter, not happy or content but manic. "Did you see her face, my boy? A picture! A picture!"

He was clearly a long way from fine.

Shortly after, Mr. Lock marshalled us in the hallway to receive our guests. Lord Greave, I was pleased to see, was fully dressed and stationed with Samuel in the front sitting room. His son looked every inch the gentleman in his clean dragoon's uniform. The clock was still chiming the five strokes of the hour as the doorbell rang.

Lizzy and I straightened up beside each other as Mr. Lock made his way ponderously to the door. She hadn't spoken to me once since the incident with the scarf.

The door opened to a draft of cold air.

Lord and Lady Ambrose stood there stiffly, their son Alexander just behind them.

"Greetings, Lock," he said.

"Sir," said Mr. Lock, bowing low and standing aside to let them enter. I saw their carriage in the road beyond, and wondered why they had bothered to use it—they only lived across the Park. Perched on the front seat was a footman wearing a woollen hat pulled low. Lizzy's eyes were turned that way too. The magnificent Henry, I guessed. Rob went out to guide the horses round into the yard.

"Best get that door closed, Lock," said Alexander, "before Jack Frost decides to make himself at home."

He was a tall young man—the whole family was tall and heavyset with very black hair. His father was much the same, though slightly stooped and with bulk turned to a great roll of fat that strained at his middle. Esme Ambrose was perhaps an inch shorter than her husband and wore a green dress with a scarf of dark red around her shoulders. Her eyes seemed to look straight through me, but that was often the way with visitors. It was improper to notice the staff.

Lizzy and I took our guests' outer garments—Lady Ambrose's fine fur coat—and I took their hats too.

"Show us to the invalid then!" said the son.

Mr. Lock gave a thin smile. I wondered how much Alex knew of Samuel's convalescence. The butler led them through to the sitting room and I heard the muffled sounds of warm greetings. Lizzy and I went to the closet beneath the stairs, where we hung the coats and hats.

"I swear to you that I didn't damage your scarf," I said.

She turned her back on me without a word.

Lizzy's spirits were shortly to be lifted by an unexpected visitor.

Mr. Lock was upstairs serving drinks in the sitting room, while the rest of us bustled around the kitchen. I was warming plates over the range and Lizzy was helping Cook put the finishing touches to the fish course—a huge poached salmon with caviar jelly.

The back door opened and in walked Rob alongside the Ambroses' footman, Henry, who quickly pulled the hat from his head and held it shyly in front of him. On his hands were fingerless gloves.

"Evening, all," he said.

"Let me get you a cup of ale," said Rob.

"I should be glad of it," said Henry.

We made our introductions briefly, and I saw his eyes linger on Lizzy longer than was proper. It made me worry for her. If Mrs. Cotton had been there, she would have been sure to note the flicker of attraction between the two of them and snuff it like a candle.

Henry seemed a nice enough young man as he supped his ale and gradually the color returned to his cheeks. Like his master, there was always a smile on his lips. He told us a little of himself—that two of his brothers were in service too, though another was apprenticed to a cobbler, that he had been with the Ambrose family for two years and that they were good to him. Lizzy hung on his every word, though I'm sure she'd heard it all before.

Shortly afterwards Mr. Lock came down to tell us the diners were seated. It was time for us to take the soup upstairs. I carried the bowls and Lizzy the tureen. We crossed the hall and Mr. Lock opened the dining-room door for us.

A fire was blazing and the lamps were all lit. The room was brighter and hotter than the rest of the house and straight away a light sweat pricked across my forehead beneath the starched hat. Lord Greave sat at the head of the table, with Samuel at his right side. Alex was beside his friend and his parents sat opposite. Only half the table was being used.

" . . . read about in the papers," Alexander was saying. "It sounded hellish."

Lizzy placed the tureen on a trolley by the near wall, and I held the first of the bowls as she ladled it in. We had done this so many times, we didn't spill or splash a drop. I served Lady Ambrose first, then her husband.

I was carrying the third bowl to their son. He moved aside to let me place it before him, but two things seemed to happen in the same moment. I felt a cold breath on the back of my neck, which sent a tingle right along my spine, and the bowl tipped out of my hand. I looked on in horror as the scalding liquid splashed into Alexander Ambrose's lap.

He screamed in pain and pushed back from the table. "Abi!" said Samuel.

I grabbed a napkin from the table and held it out to Alexander. "Sir, I apologize. I don't know what happened. I—"

Master Ambrose was hopping from foot to foot as though it was the ground that burned him, not the soup that dripped from his crotch and all over the carpet.

"You stupid girl!" he said, snatching the napkin and holding it to his nether regions. "What are you? An imbecile?"

What could I say? I wanted to run out of the room and not look back, or crawl under the table and hide. Only Mr Ambrose had stood up—the rest remained seated. I took in their aghast expressions, wishing to be anywhere but there. Even Lizzy looked appalled.

"I'm dreadfully sorry, sir," I said, imploring Lord Greave with my eyes to intervene. But he wasn't even looking at me. His eyes were fixed on the fire, as if he could see something there that no one else could.

It was Samuel who broke the silence.

"Miss Tamper," he said, with sudden formality, "you are excused. I will bring Master Ambrose's garments to you for washing and you will make sure they are cleaned and dried by morning."

I couldn't tell if his tone was for the benefit of his guests or because he was truly angry. His face gave nothing away.

"Of course, sir," I said.

"Alex," he said, "Lock will show you to the library. You will find some of my clothes hanging there. Please take what you need."

"They'll be ruined," muttered Lady Ambrose, not looking at me.

"I'll get them clean, ma'am," I said. She turned to me with a look of disgust. I shouldn't have spoken.

"I told you to go," said Samuel.

I left the room, passing Samuel and Lizzy, my cheeks burning.

As I closed the door behind me I caught a final glimpse of Lord Greave, still gazing at the hypnotic flames in the grate. Had he sensed it too—the presence that I had felt at my back just a second before the bowl fell?

I waited at the top of the servants' steps until Mr. Lock brought me a pile of soup-stained clothes. "Make sure these are spotless," he said. He was about to go, then added. "What came over you, my girl?"

"I don't know," I replied. "I must have slipped."

Mr. Lock left me, shaking his head. If he was baffled, then so was I.

I carved some soap shavings into a bucket of hot water and dropped Alexander's clothes in. Lizzy would have to deal with service for the remainder of the evening, but I thought she might enjoy it more without me there anyway. She had wanted me to spill, and spill I had, but I couldn't blame her.

"It was you, wasn't it?" I said to the empty laundry.

The soup came out easily and by the third rinse there was no sign of it. The kitchen was too thick with cooking fumes to hang the clothes beside the range, so I ran them through the mangle to get rid of most of the remaining water and took them up to my own room. With all the fires burning downstairs, the warmth had risen pleasantly through the house. With luck, they'd be almost dry by morning.

I sat on the bed to gather my thoughts. Thank goodness Mrs. Cotton hadn't been at dinner! Her absence was a small blessing that gave this otherwise grey cloud a silver lining. But I'd let Samuel down most of all, and on his special night too. Since he'd arrived home I'd cared for him like a sister, but now that good work was at least partly undone. I could hardly tell him that my mother's ghost was responsible!

I made a promise to myself to redouble my efforts the next day, and began to formulate a speech of apology to set us on the right track again.

It was only then that I realized the unexpected result of the humiliation. Not only was Mrs. Cotton safely out of the way for several hours, but I was no longer required downstairs. I suddenly felt light with excitement, and took my watch from the shelf above my bed.

Almost seven o'clock. Dr. Reinhardt would be at home.

A cold sensation crept across my skin as the possibilities became clear. Could I risk it, though? There were still a hundred other things that could trip me up. What if Cook called me down, or Mr. Lock wanted something else done? They'd find me gone and questions would be asked. Mrs. Cotton would come to know about it and then . . .

I pushed the clamor of objections aside. I could spend all night dreaming up reasons not to go. My heart felt light again.

The decision was made.

I unfastened the ties of my serving dress and pulled it over my head. If I was going to 11b Argyle Terrace, I needed to change.

Twenty-one

I MADE MY WAY DOWNSTAIRS, PAUSING EVERY FEW
steps to make sure that no one was coming. The tinkle
of cutlery and glasses trickled up the stairs from the
dining room, accompanied by muffled laughter. Clearly
my disaster was forgotten.

I wore my plain blue dress, washed clean from the
night of my failed escape. If anyone saw me now, my
attire would seem odd but not inexplicable. Still, I didn't
want to risk being seen.

On the ground floor, I heard steps coming up
from the scullery and pressed myself against the wall.
From the sound I knew it was Lizzy, probably taking
in the dessert—a great meringue flavored with vanilla
cream. I heard the dining-room door open and close
again, which meant Mr. Lock was still inside too. There
was only Cook to contend with. I crept down the back

steps into the scullery and could hear her banging pans in the kitchen. The back door was a little ajar, and I passed silently through. It wasn't as cold a night as we'd had recently, but I was glad of my long stockings. The Ambroses' carriage was unhitched in front the stable barn and their horse was lodged in a stall beside Lancelot's, covered with a thick blanket.

I was almost at the gate when I heard a voice behind me.

"Bit late to be heading out, ain't it?"

Henry was sitting on the back fender of the carriage, the red glow of a cheroot clamped between his lips. I was caught.

"Good evening," I said, trying to sound calm. "Where's Rob?"

"Gone to make sure his master's fire is well-stoked," he said. "He'll be back soon enough though, so I should go now if you have a mind to go at all."

I paused, unsure. "You mean you won't tell?" I said.

He hoisted a foot and put out the cigarette on the sole of his boot. "I've no reason to, have I?" he said.

He was smiling but it was a knowing grin, and then I understood. He knew that I knew about him and Elizabeth.

"We shall keep each other's secrets then," I said.

He nodded. "You have yourself a fine evening, little one."

I heard Rob's voice in the kitchen, and then Cook's, saying that she'd have his guts for garters. Then his feet on the loose gravel. Too late. I darted past Henry and behind the carriage.

"Look what I've found us," said Rob, laughing. "A leg of chicken each."

Henry stood up. "Come," he said. "Let's go back inside. My hands are blue."

"Then you can face Cook's wrath first," said Rob.

"Thank you," I whispered, even though he couldn't hear.

Having unlatched the gates I was out on St. Anne's Lane. Of course I hadn't a clue which way to go, but I planned to stop the nearest cabby and ask him the way. I went south, avoiding the park and threading through the smaller streets. The residences were less grand than Greave Hall, and lamps shone from many windows. It was not yet late, and the pavements were filled with men and women well wrapped up for the night. They paid little attention to me. I suppose they thought I was an errand girl, a servant rushing from one house to another to deliver a message or fetch something. Carriages of all shapes and sizes rattled up and down the roads, the horses bobbing their heads and giving snorting breaths. No stars were out, and the moon shone through the clouds like a lamp blurred behind a muslin sheet. The air was thick with the smell of a thousand fires and their smoking chimneys. I passed a boy of my age pulling a cart. He was dressed in rags but smiling anyway, and calling out, "Lovely chestnuts! Warm your hearts and fill your bellies. Lovely chestnuts!"

Finally I saw what I was after: a hackney carriage, parked and empty, with its driver checking his harnesses.

"Please, sir," I said, "I'm looking for Argyle Terrace. Could you direct me?"

He looked at me with a slight bewilderment. "Long way to be heading this time o' night. Over the river."

"I know," I said. "My sister has reached her term before we expected, and I have to fetch her mother. If you could just point the way."

He continued to give me an odd look, and I thought he must have seen through my lie. But then he nodded to the cab.

"Listen, lassie, I live not far from there myself. Jump

in and I'll take you there now."

I wasn't used to kindnesses of any sort, so my first thought was to refuse. He saw my hesitation.

"You've barely got a stitch on. It's a good mile, and not an easy route."

"Very well," I said. "Thank you."

And so it was that, having never before moved anywhere but with the power of my own feet, I took a cab ride over Vauxhall Bridge. We passed Millbank prison to the left, lying squat and unlit by the river. The driver was kind enough not to probe me further on my pregnant sister, and busied himself steering his horses with clucks and whistles, and twitches on the reins.

The bridge was illuminated by lamps, which reflected in the snaking black river beneath. A mist thickened a few yards above the road, but the way was clear and I stared, open-mouthed, at the great city stretching to the east. I could see the majestic towers of Westminster and the dome of St. Paul's. The river itself was clogged with craft—barges and fishing boats, rowing boats and sailing ships.

Once we reached the other side, I forced myself to focus on the route we were taking. My temporary escape would be pointless if I couldn't find my way home. We left the main road and made a series of turns, passing a steepled church and small park garden. After less than ten minutes I saw the sign: *Argyle Terrace*.

"We're here," I said over the clatter of the horses' hooves.

"What number would you like?" said the driver.

I told him, and he jockeyed the horses on a few more yards. The terraced houses here were nothing like Park Avenue, the road narrower and broken up at the edges.

I saw the number 11.

"I'm sorry that I cannot pay you," I said.

"Never mind that," he said. "I hope your sister keeps her good health and the baby is a bonnie one."

I jumped down from the cab and walked to the door. If this was 11, where was 11b? The cab driver had still not pulled away, and seemed to be waiting for me to be safe inside. I took a guess and opened the small gate in the railings—a flight of stone steps led to another door below street level. Sure enough, the door was marked "11b."

I knocked.

The driver had still not moved off, and I gave him a little wave. He nodded back.

The door opened, and there stood Dr. Reinhardt.

He looked rather less dapper than the last time I'd

seen him. He wasn't wearing a jacket or tie, but instead a sleeveless jumper with his collar open. A pair of reading spectacles was balanced on his nose.

"Can I help you?" he asked.

I was glad to hear the carriage move off.

He obviously didn't recognize me. Why should he? The last time he'd looked at me, he had been in some strange trance. And afterwards he had been so perturbed, I doubted he would remember any of the faces from Greave Hall apart from Mrs. Cotton's.

"I'm Abigail Tamper," I said.

He frowned as though the name meant nothing to him, then his eyebrows lifted.

"Of course! Miss Tamper. That odd little letter without an address! Ah—I expected—"

I smiled. "Someone older?"

He took off his glasses hurriedly, and swept an arm inside. "Please, do come in."

Twenty-two

DR. REINHARDT'S HOME WAS HUMBLE IN comparison to Greave Hall, but more cozy by far. He showed me along a narrow corridor, at the end of which I could see a dark kitchen, and into a front parlor little bigger than my own bedroom. A fire blazed in the hearth and after being outside, it was almost suffocatingly warm. He gestured to a pot on the table.

"Would you like some tea? I've just made some."

"Yes, please," I said. He seemed a mile away from the formal gentleman who'd come to Greave Hall. While he fetched another cup from an ancient dresser, I had a chance to inspect the room. The walls were covered in paintings and framed maps, almost all hanging slightly cock-eyed, as if the room had suffered a minor earth tremor and not been straightened since. Apart from the chair I sat on, there was a couch, a small table containing an empty vase and a simple three-legged stool. Ornaments and other curiosities crowded the dresser and mantelpiece. I saw a stuffed bat, a book no larger than the palm of my hand, and a wooden mask, elongated and severe, with dark slashes for eyes and what looked like real hair stitched into its upper rim.

Dr. Reinhardt saw me staring and pulled it down.

"A shaman's tool," he said. "I found it on my travels to Africa."

I knew of the place, for I'd seen it on a map, but asked what a shaman was.

"It's a sort of witch doctor, and with the mask he claims to see to the other side." He spoke the words with the hint of a smile.

"Have you . . ." I began. "Can you see the other side with it?"

The doctor shook his head as he poured. "Not with that. We all have our different methods. Which I suppose," he paused to hand me the cup and saucer, "is why you're here?"

His eyes were kind as he looked over his spectacles, and I tried to gather my thoughts. I'd dwelled so long on the impossibility of my ever getting here that I hadn't thought through exactly what I would say when I did.

"You cannot say anything that will surprise me," he said.

So I told him the truth. "I wish to talk to my mother."

"She has passed away?" he asked.

"A year ago."

He leaned back in his chair. "Miss Tamper, I understand your grief and I'm sorry for your loss. Many come to me wanting to reconnect with those who have left us. But have you stopped to think that perhaps your mother is content wherever she may now be?"

"I don't think she is content," I said, taking a sip of tea. "You see, she's been doing things."

"Things?" asked the doctor, suddenly intrigued.

"Moving objects, frightening me," I said. "She seems . . . angry."

"And do you know what might have angered her?"

Did I dare to speak the word that had escaped his own lips? The dreaded word "murder"?

"No," I said. "I thought you might be able to help me find out."

The doctor walked to the small window and stood with his back to me. The curtains were only half drawn, but little light could have entered those basement rooms even on the brightest day of summer. "Sometimes," he said, "the spirits themselves are confused. They want to join us, and to take part in the activities they enjoyed while alive, but they cannot. The boundaries between this world and the next are like oil and water. They cannot exist together, but pools can form, pockets where one exists inside the other. If they have left something unsaid or undone in life, it's through these pockets that they come back to haunt us. What you see as your mother's anger may simply be her confused spirit trying to find its way through."

"And you can ease her passage?" I said.

He pulled the curtains tightly closed.

"I can," he said. "Have you on your person some object that belonged to her?"

I hadn't, and said so.

"Then you must come again," he said, "and bring something."

"No," I said, without thinking. "I can't come again. It must be tonight."

A look of impatience flashed across the doctor's face. He had no idea how difficult tonight had been, how only through a year's worth of luck had I been able to leave the house at all.

"I have stipulated the conditions," he said. "I'm not a conjuror who can magic your mother's ghost into this room."

"I'm sorry," I said. "I'm desperate. It won't be possible for me to leave the house a second time."

He looked at me oddly then, and I knew his kindness was evaporating into suspicion.

"I recognize your face, I think," he said. "You are a servant, are you not? At that big house by the Park."

"No," I said quickly. Too quickly.

"As well as being a medium," said the doctor, "I'm also an expert in the signals of lying." His eyes narrowed. "Yes, I remember you more clearly now. I had a strange turn there, in that room. You were beside me as I woke. Your employer has sent you, has she?"

The game was up, and I knew I didn't have the skill to continue the deception.

"I only want to speak to my mother," I pleaded.

"Without a token, I can no more speak to her than any other corpse that lies in the ground," he said harshly. "Now, please leave me and stop wasting my time."

The shaman's mask eyed me from the mantel.

"Is there no other way?" I said.

The doctor waved his hand. "There are countless ways to talk to the dead," he said, "but they will all cost you, and I take it that I have been duped and you have no money."

I felt wretched and suddenly tired. My high hopes on leaving Greave Hall, bolstered by the generosity of the cab driver and the magnificent sights of the city, now lay in shattered ruins. The doctor was standing at the parlor door, tapping his foot. I stood up, then felt a weight in my pocket: my father's watch.

I pulled it out.

"I have this," I said, before even thinking through the implications. The doctor's eyes lighted on the timepiece, and he held out his hand.

"Let me see," he said.

I handed it to him. "It belonged to my father."

He turned the watch over. I knew enough to be certain it had value, but he sniffed. "It's broken."

"It can't be," I said. "I wind it every night."

"Well," he said, "it's stopped now." He fiddled with the winder and tossed it back to me. I caught the watch and looked at the face. He was right. The second hand was still, the time was well off.

"I don't understand . . ." my words dried up in my throat. My eyes checked the hands again. It wasn't the fact that the watch had stopped but the position of those hands that held me. Seventeen minutes past four.

"Well, it's time you left," the doctor said. "Otherwise I will have to have serious words with your employer— something which I expect you would care to avoid."

Seventeen minutes past four. The time, to the exact minute, when my mother had died.

"It can be fixed," I said, holding it out. "Please, is there's anything you can do to help me?"

He looked at me for a good five seconds without speaking, then sighed. "Very well," he said, "but I will hear no more of you after today." He opened a cupboard and took out what looked like a dirty rolled-up tablecloth.

He crouched down and spread it out on the floor.

It wasn't as big as a tablecloth, and was circular in shape. Around the edges were the embroidered letters of the alphabet, and between the letters *Z* and *A* were stitched the words "Aye" and "No."

"What is it?" I asked.

"They call it a Ouija," he said.

I must have given him a blank look.

"It's another method to talk to those who are no longer in this world."

I was skeptical—it looked like something a child would make under a nurse's care.

"How does it work?" I asked.

Dr. Reinhardt took an empty cup from the dresser. "Find a quiet place," he said, "then take a pointer— you'll need something round that rolls easily." He turned the cup upside down in the center of the cloth. "Sit down and place your fingers like this," he went on, touching his index and middle fingers to the top of the cup.

"And then?"

"Then ask your questions."

I laughed a little. It looked so foolish.

"Do you want it or not?" he said, his anger bubbling to the surface once more.

What else was there? I nodded.

"Then give me the watch. A broken timepiece is a fair price."

Reluctantly, I handed back the watch. He rolled up the cloth and gave it to me, then led the way to the front door. He held it open.

"Goodbye, Miss Tamper. I hope you find what you're looking for."

"So do I," I replied, stepping out into the cold. The mist had dropped further now, and drifted along the road.

I climbed the steps. "I say, my girl!" the doctor called after me.

I turned. "Yes?"

"You say this watch belonged to your father."

"It did," I said. "He was apprenticed to a clockmaker."

"Why do you speak of him in the past?"

"He's dead, sir, these many years."

Dr. Reinhardt rubbed his thumb over the watch's surface, as though he could feel something there, some grain or mark invisible to the naked eye.

"How strange," he said. "Normally I can tell."

He closed the door.

Twenty-three

THE WAY BACK WAS EASIER THAN I EXPECTED. With the Ouija clutched to my chest, I crossed the bridge again. The mist had dropped to ground level and I could no longer make out the water below. It was like walking in the clouds.

I already regretted losing the watch, not so much for myself but because it would have upset my mother. Her eyes had misted over the few times I'd mentioned my father, and it had been my only remaining connection to him. But with no memories attached to it, no face or voice filled with love, it was really just an object. I couldn't help thinking that the marked cloth in my hands was infinitely more valuable now.

On leaving Argyle Terrace I walked quickly, driven by my anger towards Dr. Reinhardt. I was stupid and naive to think that he might help me for nothing as the cab driver had. Things could have ended far worse, with a letter to Mrs. Cotton, but I suspected then that I would never see or hear from him again.

As I neared Greave Hall my anger lifted, replaced by a rising tide of fear. I dropped my head, lest any of the neighbors recognize me, and crossed the road when I saw pedestrians approaching. To be caught now, or even seen, could spell disaster. The lights of the dining room had been extinguished, and as I crept along the side passage by the house, I heard noises outside the back door. I crouched beside the gatepost and peered in.

Henry was busy with the Ambroses' carriage in the yard. Luck was on my side, for it meant that they were in the process of leaving, and attention—at least that of most of the household—would be focused on the front door. I pressed myself into the shadows beside a bush as the carriage shambled out of the gate. When it was well clear, I streaked across the yard and back down the steps into the scullery.

"Is that you, Rob?" said Cook from the kitchen.

Rowena came out first, and I realized she must have been looking for food. Cook followed, drying her hands on a towel, and I quickly put the cloth behind my back.

"Oh, Abi," she said. "I thought you were in bed long ago."

"I left my sewing down here," I said, quickly flashing the cloth.

Rowena suddenly arched her back and hissed.

"What's wrong with you, silly thing?" said Cook. "Well, Abi, mind you don't throw any of my best soup over it."

She waddled back into kitchen, laughing softly to herself.

I could hear noises at the top of the servants' stairs. I looked around quickly for somewhere to hide the cloth and realized there was only one sure place and it was beneath my feet. I stepped aside and bent over, yanking at the iron ring on the trapdoor. It shifted a few inches. Lord, it was heavy! I managed to drop the cloth inside, behind some crates, and let it down again just as Mr. Lock came in, carrying some cups on a tray. He took in my dress.

"You shouldn't be dressed like that down here," he said. "If Mrs. Cotton catches you—"

"She won't," I said, stepping past him to the stairs. "I'm going straight back up."

He tutted and let me go.

I lit a taper at the lamp halfway up and cradled it in my hand as I climbed the attic stairs. There was no light from under Lizzy's door, so it was very dark. It must have been close to nine thirty. She was either in bed already or still downstairs, cleaning up.

I opened my own door and almost screamed. There, on my bed, lay a black shape. As the light from the taper spread, I realized it was Elizabeth. She was shaking a little and sobbing quietly.

"Lizzy?" I said, leaning forward and lighting a candle. "Whatever's the matter?"

She slowly sat up and looked at me with bloodshot, dark-fringed eyes.

"Oh, Abi," she said, putting her arms around me and holding me tight.

I let her hug me, my mind racing. What could be wrong with her? My first thought was that her sister must have died. Or perhaps the baby.

I pulled away and held her face between my hands. "What's happened?" I asked gently.

Her face creased again. "It's Henry," she said.

Relief flooded through me, and I was glad to hold her head against my shoulder in case she saw my expression. I knew he was alive and well, so it could only be . . .

"He says we cannot see each other any more," she said. "He says it's not proper."

"Oh, Lizzy," I said. I remembered his easy way down by the gate, and how he had helped me to run away when he didn't have to. He had asked me to keep his secret too, and yet he had been planning all along to end it like this. It was callous, but perhaps he had seen sense. There would be other men for Lizzy, when she was more established.

"I didn't know who else to come to," Lizzy sobbed, "but I couldn't find you."

"I'm sorry," I said. "I'm here now. It's for the best, Lizzy."

She turned her red-rimmed eyes on me and said, "Oh, but you don't understand."

We stayed like that for some minutes, until her tears were exhausted. My mind turned to other things, such as how I would get the cloth back from the cellar. I decided that the early morning was my best opportunity, before anyone else was up. I let Lizzy come in with me again that night, turning over the pillow that she had soaked with her crying. While she drifted off to sleep, I couldn't. Down there, in the darkness, was the key to speaking to my mother.

Fate conspired against me on the following day. Cook was already bustling around as I came down, and when she went to use the privy Mrs. Cotton appeared, much earlier than was usual for her. It was as though she half-knew my secret purpose and meant to foil me.

Alexander Ambrose visited twice on the day after the dinner party. He and Samuel sat alone in the library during the late morning, and I could hear their occasional laughter while I was cleaning the downstairs rooms. Mr. Lock was working harder than usual, attending to the frequent bell, and it was clear, at least to me, that he was struggling with his duties.

Then, in the afternoon, while I was trying not to dwell on the frustration of not being able to get into the cellar, Master Ambrose arrived at the front door with a chair on wheels. Samuel gave a whoop as he sat in it and wheeled himself about with his hands. I thought he was so brave to count such a thing a blessing after his great loss.

With his spirits lifted, the house began slowly to return to normal. The next day, I was sent upstairs in the afternoon to prepare Samuel's old bedroom. He'd made it clear that he was not to be treated like an invalid any longer, and meant "to live on the second floor, like any gentleman."

The bed was dismantled again and carried upstairs once more, and I cleaned the carpets and furniture with pride. His room offered a fine view over the park opposite, and I could see Alexander pushing him in his chair under the bare trees and towards the lake. At one point, Alexander turned back to the house and seemed to take it all in. His face wore an oddly serious expression. Then he nodded, and they continued on their walk.

"You aren't paid to stare out of the window," said a voice behind me.

Mrs. Cotton stood in the doorway.

Not a week ago, the look would have chilled me. But now I looked at her, not defiantly, but not cowed either.

"Yes, ma'am."

I picked up a vase to take downstairs.

"Where do you think you're going with that?" Mrs. Cotton said.

"Master Greave has requested some fresh flowers, ma'am, to brighten up his room."

Her mouth twisted. "Lilies, I suppose?"

Her words, and the sly smile that accompanied them, were weighted to hurt me. Lilies had been my mother's favorite.

"No, ma'am," I said. "Not this time of year."

She moved aside. "Well, be quick about it," she snapped.

I was shaking as I filled the vase with water.

Twenty-four

THOUGH SAMUEL'S HEALTH SEEMED TO BE improving, the same couldn't be said for Lord Greave. He took to dining alone again in his room, and when Mr. Lock descended the stairs that evening with the tray and decanter, the glass beside it was in pieces. I was in the kitchen, hoping that I might get a moment alone to retrieve the precious object under the scullery floor, but Rob seemed happy fiddling with a chair that needed mending. I made myself busy at the range, sweeping out the old ashes.

"He's bad again, is he?" asked Rob.

Mr. Lock nodded gravely, then looked at me as though unsure what he could or should say. "He's seeing things, hearing things."

My ears pricked.

"Perhaps you should tell the young master," said Rob. "He may know what to do."

"Perhaps," grunted Mr. Lock. "Abi, fetch me a cloth and bucket, will you? There's a mess up there."

"Send Miss Tamper to clean it up," said Mrs. Cotton.

She had drifted in from the main stairs without us noticing. She was wearing a grey housecoat.

"But madam," said Mr. Lock, "His Lordship—"

"Mr. Lock," she said, "you look terribly tired. My brother won't object, I'm sure."

I looked uncertainly at Mr. Lock. It was rare for Mrs. Cotton and he to clash, as they went about their duties with little need to confer. His Lordship's chamber was, according to custom, the butler's domain, while cleaning jobs fell to the housekeeper.

"Very well," said Mr. Lock.

I couldn't find the silver pail, and no one seemed to have seen it, so I filled a jug with water and took it up to the top floor. I knocked, of course, and Lord Greave bade me enter. He was seated in his armchair by the window, wearing his dressing gown and smoking a pipe. If I hadn't seen the shattered glass and heard Mr. Lock's report, I would have thought him like any other contented gentleman, enjoying the last hours before retiring.

However, on the carpet was a wet patch and

fragments of broken glass. I set about picking them up and dabbing the carpet with salted water to soak up the stain. He didn't speak a word, and it wasn't my place to initiate conversation. I was sponging at a particularly stubborn patch in uncomfortable silence when he spoke.

"She did it," he said.

I looked up, unsure if I had heard correctly. "Excuse me, sir?"

"It wasn't me," he said, more quietly this time.

He wasn't looking at me, but staring towards the black glass of the window. I could see his reflection in it.

"Do you mean broke the glass, sir?" I said. "That's no matter."

"She's angry," he said.

It's strange how fear works. It suddenly stands at your shoulder, and slides its arm around you. Its fist closes on your heart.

"Who's she, sir?"

He turned then, and focused his pale blue eyes on me. They were full of tears.

"There was nothing I could do. You understand that, don't you, Susan?"

I stood up sharply. "Abigail, sir. Susan was my mother."

He raised his hand and buried his head in it. His shoulders shook with crying.

I picked up my things and quit the room.

I went into the scullery again to empty the pail. The back door clicked open, and in rushed Rowena.

Behind her came Mrs. Cotton. Her cheeks were flushed, and I thought it was with the cold.

"Look who I found," she said. "I thought we'd lost our devious little mouser."

Rowena rushed up the servants' stairs. She wanted to get back to her kittens, no doubt.

"Oh, I'm glad," I said.

Mrs. Cotton closed the door. "And how is His Lordship? I trust you cleared up the mess."

I wasn't sure which question to answer, so I said it was all clean now.

She hesitated, and I saw there was something she wanted to say. A feeling grew that I wouldn't like whatever it was.

I dried my hands. "Will there be anything else, ma'am?"

She shook her head. The silence was disconcerting.

I went to the bottom of the stairs.

"Oh, Abigail?" she said.

I paused. "Yes, ma'am?"

"You were looking for the silver pail, weren't you?"

"I was, ma'am."

She opened the back door again. "I thought I saw it in the stable store. Perhaps you could fetch it in."

I went out of the scullery and into the yard. It was very dark, a mild night under heavy cloud. It was hard to see anything in the store, but Mrs. Cotton was right. The pail was at the back of the little chamber. I picked it up by the handle and found it heavy. Water sloshed over the edge. I carried it outside to empty into the drain.

Only outside did I see there was something floating on top. It looked like three rags.

I screamed and dropped the bucket in the yard. Water spilled out towards the drain in the center and the three little cats fell damply onto the cobbles.

Mrs. Cotton stood at the back door. Her face was cast in shadow, but I could feel her smiling.

Twenty-five

BACK IN MY ROOM, LIT ONLY BY THE DIM GLOW from a candle, I cried. I felt completely powerless and the injustice boiled within me, making me lightheaded. There was nothing I could do to stop her, no one I could speak to. She was cruel but she was clever, too. I doubted that Sammy would bat an eyelid at the drowning of the kittens. What use were they, after all? He wouldn't see that the only reason Mrs. Cotton had killed them was to hurt me. And for what reason except that she could?

I ground my fists into my pillow to control my anger. I could almost feel my mother watching me. If only I could see her again! If only I could smell her skin or touch her soft cheek! I would have given everything I had for just a minute alone with her, face to face, to be able to slip my hands around her and breathe her in.

Something—anything—would be enough.

I lay on my bed and watched the candle flame burn.

"If you're here," I whispered, "blow out the flame."

I watched, but it didn't even flicker.

"Please," I begged. "Show me."

I focused all my mind on the candle, as though willpower alone could extinguish the fire.

My eyes began to sting and I blinked away the tears that had appeared.

Why couldn't she do this one little thing for me? She could throw plates and glasses, she could leave handprints on the windows and toy with me in countless ways.

I blew out the candle with an angry puff.

It must have been the creak of the floor that woke me. My eyes seemed blinded by light, and I threw up my arms to shield them. It came from a lantern. A figure stood over my bed.

"Where is it?" hissed the voice.

"What?" I mumbled, my voice thick with sleep.

It was Mrs. Cotton. Her eyes blazed. She bared

her teeth and hissed. "You know what, you little horror. Where's the key?"

I tried to roll away, but she seized my arm and pulled me off the bed. I cried out as my knees grazed the floor, but she kept hold of me and tugged me up. Her strength was incredible.

"You will tell me now where it is, or I swear I will beat you until your skin is nothing but ribbons," she said.

My head swam with dizziness. The light, the sudden jolt from sleep, the pain in my wrist and knees—all threatened to overcome me. "Please!" I gasped. "I don't know."

She released me and I fell back against the bed. My thoughts were confused. "The key to what?" I said.

"Tell me!" she shouted. The lantern threw thick shadows trembling across the little room. "The library key!"

My mind found some focus. The library key? The key for the French windows leading to the garden? I said the first thing I could think of. "Maybe Samuel—"

Her hand came down in the darkness like a swooping bird, and cracked across my cheek. "You will not lie to me, child!" She reached down and pulled the keys from her pocket. I couldn't speak. My face felt like it was on fire. She jangled the keys in front of my eyes. "Taken from this very ring. You dare to blame my nephew for this?"

"I—I—"

She lifted her hand again, but then a voice spoke from behind her.

"What's the matter, ma'am?"

Lizzy stood in the doorway, smoothing her nightdress.

Mrs. Cotton lowered her arm. "It's nothing that concerns you," she said. "Go back to bed."

Lizzy didn't move.

Mrs. Cotton turned on her. "I will not repeat myself."

Lizzy retreated, looking down at me with concern. She went into her own room across the hall, but didn't close the door.

Mrs. Cotton seemed to think better of continuing her assault, and pointed a bony finger at me.

"You got away once, Abigail Tamper, but you will not do so again. I will die before I see you escape this house."

"I swear it wasn't me," I said.

She reached over me and pulled the comforter off my bed. With both hands she searched desperately among the sheets. Then she went to the chest and flung open the lid. She rooted through it, but I knew she would find nothing. I watched her back as she ferreted. Anger surged through me, and words gathered behind my teeth like a great flood behind a dam. I could say it now. I could say that I knew what she'd done. That she was a murderer.

The words were ready, but I couldn't utter them.

My tongue twisted around the phrases, and what finally escaped was quite different.

"Why did you hate her?" I asked.

Breathless, she stood and retrieved her lamp. She didn't look at me as her chest rose and fell. "I will find it," she said, "and when I do . . ."

She left the room, pulling the door closed as she went. I listened to her heavy tread descend the stairs.

I remade the bed and lay on it. My tongue played inside my mouth. The blow had loosened a tooth slightly.

The key had nothing to do with me. Someone else had taken it, but I didn't really care who.

I remembered the bolt drawn across the coal store on New Year's Day, seemingly by an invisible hand. But there was a big difference between moving a bolt and taking a key off a ring, wasn't there?

My door opened and Lizzy came in.

"Are you all right?" she asked, sitting on my bed and resting a hand on my foot.

There was a time when I would have cried, as I had cried on her shoulder countless times over the past year.

"I didn't take her blasted key," I said. "And I didn't

tear your scarf either."

"I know you didn't," she said kindly.

I sat up and hugged her.

"It'll be all right though, you'll see," she said sadly. "As long as we stick together."

Lizzy was the best friend I ever had. I decided it was time to tell her what I knew. About my mother. About the happenings. About what I suspected Mrs. Cotton had done.

But I realized my shoulder was wet. She was crying. How selfish I was, thinking about myself when she had her own problems!

"Is it Henry?" I asked.

She sniffed loudly and nodded. I searched for something to say.

"There'll be someone else. Someone who deserves you."

"It's not that," she said, wiping her eyes.

"What is it then?"

She smiled. Such a sad smile.

"I'm pregnant."

She dissolved into tears after that. I waited until she had finished, and it gave me time to think. "Are you sure?" I asked.

"I am," she said. "I missed my time. Most mornings

I've felt dreadful. My sister went through it just the same."

I remembered her being sick but I hadn't realized it happened so regularly.

"And it's Henry's?" I said.

Her eyes widened. "Who else?"

They'd done much more than kiss, then.

"What will you do?"

That made her cry again. Good work, Abigail! I was about to ask if Henry knew himself, but then I understood.

"That's why he broke it off, isn't it?" I said.

She blew her nose on a handkerchief. "He said he can't afford a family."

And neither can you, I thought grimly. We'd all heard stories of staff who were found to be with child. It was back to their folks, normally. But Lizzy only had her sister.

There was little more for either of us to say, and she went back to bed. As the door I told her, truthfully, that I couldn't tell her condition by looking at her. She was only a few weeks gone and it would be several months before she showed enough for Mrs. Cotton, or any of the others, to be sure.

As it was, she had much less time than we thought.

Twenty-six

FOR THE FIRST TIME SINCE I COULD REMEMBER,
I overslept the next morning. When I woke, my hand
reached automatically for the watch before I remembered
that it wasn't there. I dressed and rushed downstairs,
knowing that I was late, but not by how much.

Cook was already up and the fires were lit under the
range.

"Don't worry yourself," she said. "She's not down yet,
and she shan't hear from me."

Cook looked even more ragged then usual that
morning. Her face was puffy and covered in red blotches
and her eyes ringed with yellowish skin. As she brushed
past me carrying a dustpan, a wave of stale air followed
her. I wondered if she had been drinking since she awoke.

"Miss McMahon," I asked, "have you seen anything
odd of late? Around the house."

"And what would you be meaning by odd?" she asked. She came up to me, and her careworn face was alive with anxiety. I'd struck a nerve.

"It's only that . . ." I began. Should I really be confiding in her? She'd think me mad. "Oh, it's nothing," I said. "Don't mind me."

She gripped my arm, not hard like Mrs. Cotton the night before, but firmly enough.

"Odd, you say?"

Something in her look frightened me, so I pulled my arm away. "No. I'm being silly."

I walked over the trapdoor on my way to light the fires in the main rooms. Down there was the key to this oddness. I wouldn't oversleep tomorrow.

Weariness dogged me all morning. I did my best to avoid Mrs. Cotton, and when I couldn't, I tried to be in the company of others when we met.

Cook had seen something, I was sure. She'd latched on to me as though we were two people lost in a storm. Lizzy's expression was mournful, and Lord Greave didn't come down at all. Mr. Lock went about the house like a man in a daze. It was as if the ghost was haunting all of us.

Adam arrived at the backyard after lunch as I was drying the plates. He was drawing the coal wagon that day, and I unbolted the hatch from the inside, then went out to sign for it.

"Mornin'," he said. "Any post for me today?"

I shot a look back at the house. "Shh!" I said. "Keep your voice down, will you?"

I'd snapped more than I meant to, and he looked hurt. "Sorry," he said.

"So you should be," I said. "I told you it was a secret, didn't I?"

I could hear my words and hated myself for it, but the frustrations of the previous days—of being stuck in that house, powerless and forever at the whim of Mrs. Cotton—bubbled over like a boiling pan, sizzling and hissing.

He grumbled something under his breath, then said, "I'll be on my way then."

"Yes, go," I said, staring at a point between him and the house.

He jumped back up on to the cart and flicked the reins. As he trundled towards the gate, I went after him to close it. "Adam," I called, "I'm sorry. I didn't mean . . ."

I'm not sure if he heard me above the clop of the horse's hooves, but he didn't look back.

The day did not improve. It was the time of week when we cleaned the unused rooms. Mrs. Cotton wouldn't go in at all, so it was Lizzy and I who went up with the brushes and polishes. We did the bedroom together, then Lizzy went to tackle the adjoining nursery.

As soon as she walked in, she backed out of the door again, with her hand clasped over her mouth.

She looked at me then back into the room once more. I dropped the brush I was holding.

"What's the matter, Lizzy?"

She was speechless. I crossed to her side and looked in. It was my turn to suck in a shocked breath.

"Who would do such a thing?" she asked.

The cot-bed was upturned and the blankets were in disarray. Samuel's toy soldiers had been flung across the floor and a spinning top lay on its side in the middle of the floor. The few storybooks had been pulled from the little shelf and hurled to the ground. It looked as if a whirlwind had passed through the room.

"Who?" said Lizzy again.

I had a good idea, but shook my head. "I don't know."

"We have to tell Mrs. Cotton," said Lizzy. She turned to the hallway, but I managed to get a hand on her shoulder.

"No!" I said. "Wait a moment."

"But she must know," said Lizzy. "Someone in the house has done this." Her expression hardened.

"I know who, and you can't say."

"Who?"

"Please," I said. "Sit down."

She looked uncertain, but did as I asked. I closed the door to the bedroom so no one could hear. I'd kept the secret until now, but I needed to tell her. I could trust her.

"Can you keep a secret?" I asked her.

She gave a worried grin, and nodded briskly. "You know I can, Abi. We're friends."

So I took a deep breath and told her everything, from the hand at the window that night to my visit to Dr. Reinhardt south of the river. It felt good to be getting it off my chest, and as the events spilled out, a great weight was lifted. I should have told her long before, and wondered what had stopped me.

Lizzy listened patiently, nodding occasionally, and her eyes stared into mine with a look of growing astonishment. It was only as I concluded my story that I found out it wasn't the story that horrified her, it was me.

She stood up from the bed where we were sitting. She looked into the room again and then at me. She was biting her lip and shaking her head.

"You don't believe me?" I asked.

"Believe you?" she cried, tears gathering in her eyes. "Abi, what a horrid trick!"

"What? No. It's no trick!"

I tried to reach for her, but she pulled away.

"What's wrong with you?" she said. "How could you make up such things about something so serious?"

Her look was one of sympathy mingled with confusion. It wasn't supposed to be like this. She had to believe me!

"It's her," I said. "You must see that."

"It's you!" she said, pointing at me. Then she laughed despairingly, wiping the tears from her eyes. "I forgave you for tearing my scarf like that. You were jealous, that's all. I know now that Henry wasn't the man I thought, but at least he had the honesty to admit his faults. At least . . ." she trailed off.

I too was crying now. "Please, Lizzy. I know it's hard to understand, but why would I lie? My mother is here. Now."

Lizzy's brow was creased and she backed away to the door.

"You really believe what you're saying, don't you?"

My throat was dry. "Of course I do."

"I won't tell, Abi," she said, nodding towards the

nursery. "I promise."

"And you'll help me?" I asked. "To find who killed my mother?"

Lizzy shook her head sadly. "I can't," she said. "And you must stop this, Abi. It's all in your mind."

She rushed from the room, leaving me more alone than ever.

Twenty-seven

WHY HAD I TOLD HER? And what did I expect would be the result? That she would say, "Yes, Abi, your mother was murdered and her ghost can't find its rest until the culprit is punished"?

She thought I was insane! And who wouldn't?

I sank down on the floor. I'd been such a fool.

Stupid, stupid, stupid!

Laughter trickled from the lower floors—Samuel's rich baritone and Alexander's snorts. At least someone in Greave Hall was happy.

For a long while I sat there alone. I felt like giving up completely. As the minutes ticked by, I asked myself how I ever could have dreamt of finding, let along proving, foul play. Mrs. Cotton's plan was foolproof, her secret buried with my mother more than a year ago.

The time for alibis was long past. Even confronted

with her deed, I could imagine her stony face and lips curled with contempt. There would be no choice other than to cast me out. Or worse, throw me in some lunatic asylum with the other poor souls tormented by fantasies.

I stood up weakly. That was it then.

"Enough," I said under my breath. "I tried."

If I expected a draft to blow across the room, signalling some displeasure from beyond the grave, then I was disappointed. The only sounds were crockery rattling in the rooms below and more guffaws from Sammy and his guest.

There was still the nursery to clean. I shook myself, and straightened my apron. I took stock.

Mrs. Cotton had always despised me and always would. I thought I might be able to repair my friendship with Lizzy, short-lived though it would be if she was thrown out. She'd told me to try and forget about it, but we both knew that was impossible. I felt ashamed even to face her again, but working below stairs that would be inevitable. At least I still had Sammy. He'd be there for me, just as I had been there for him.

I walked back into the nursery. When I entered, my legs almost gave way beneath me. "What?" I gasped.

The room was pristine. I walked into the center,

turning a full circle to take it all in.

The rocking horse was righted, the toy soldiers stood in neat ranks. The sheets on the cot were folded back and the books were aligned on their shelves.

I looked back to the main room. Had someone come in while I was musing? Perhaps Lizzy had returned and restored the room without me noticing.

But of course it wasn't that! The nursery hadn't merely been put to rights again, it was as though it had never been touched.

I still checked under the cot, as if someone might be hiding there.There was nobody. I went to the window. It was closed. Finally—and I don't know what it was that drew my eyes upwards—I looked at the ceiling hatch and suddenly felt all the breath leave my body.

There, quite clear in an otherwise spotless room, was a handprint, splayed out just like the mark on the library window many nights before. There weren't any acrobats in the house as far as I knew, which left only one other option. But why leave a handprint at all unless it was some sort of message?

No, this was meant as a message just for me, from Mama. It said, more clearly than ever, *I'm here. I'm watching over you.*

So much for a draft blowing across the room.

The incident redoubled my determination. Samuel took dinner with Alexander Ambrose again that night, with his father retreating once more to his chamber. I had a moment of panic when Rob went down to the cellar to fetch a bottle of wine, but he came up again swiftly, and I was fairly sure he hadn't spotted the item I wanted to keep hidden.

Had Mrs. Cotton asked Sammy about the library key? I wondered. If it had been just the two gentlemen I might have had a chance to ask him directly, but Mrs. Cotton chose to dine with them, so I couldn't risk it.

From what I could gather while stoking the fire in the dining room and carrying away the plates, dinner was a muted affair.

At one point during the serving of the main course of stuffed pork chops, Samuel spoke up.

"Auntie," he said—in a faintly mocking tone, I noted—"how would you like to pose for us later?"

"Pose?" she said, as though the meat she'd bitten into was rotten.

"That's right," said Samuel. "Alex here's brought over one of those dagger . . . What are they called, old chap?"

"Daguerreotypes," said Alexander, dabbing his lips with a napkin.

"Sounds vicious," said Mrs. Cotton. "What is it?"

"Oh, Auntie, don't look so suspicious," said Samuel. "It's a sort of camera. Don't you remember? They were all the rage at Crystal Palace."

I smiled to myself. I remembered the day well, four years earlier. It had been a reminder that Sammy and I weren't quite the brother and sister I'd hoped. The family—Mrs. Cotton, Lord Greave and Samuel—had gone out to the Great Exhibition with the Ambroses, while my mother and I were left indoors. She'd taken me around the Park to lessen the disappointment, and bought me an ice cream.

"Pray, what is a man of the law doing with such a contraption?" asked Mrs. Cotton.

"It's just a hobby," said Alexander anxiously. I noticed, as I carried apple sauce to the table, that Mrs. Cotton seemed to be able to reduce even grown men to nervous wrecks.

"We might take a couple of portraits in the house tomorrow, then give the thing a whirl in the garden," Samuel continued.

Mrs. Cotton pursed her lips. "Are you sure you're quite well enough to be gallivanting outside?"

Samuel grinned. "We shall hardly be gallivanting. Lots of sitting about, actually. It takes a good few minutes to fix everything up."

"Be that as it may," she said, "you must be careful, in your condition."

"You don't want to sit for us then?" said Samuel, his eyes alive with playfulness. "Be immortalized for all posterity?"

"Certainly not," said Mrs. Cotton. "Besides, I don't have a 'good few minutes' for 'sitting around.'"

Samuel chuckled, which only made Mrs. Cotton's eyes blaze brighter.

"Well, gentlemen," she said, and her voice was heavy with sarcasm, "I must retire."

"But you've hardly eaten a thing," said Samuel.

He was right. Mrs. Cotton's plate was still full.

"I've lost my appetite," she said. "Excuse me."

After she'd left the room, Samuel shook his head.

"Dear, oh dear. Seems I upset the old crone, doesn't it?"

Alexander grunted and looked at me uncomfortably.

"Oh, don't mind her," said Samuel. "She's practically one of the family."

Alexander looked less than convinced. "Been on the receiving end of Mrs. Cotton's tongue more than once, I dare say," Samuel continued. "Isn't that right, Abi?"

I smiled, but didn't speak. To do so in front of Alexander would have been out of turn. Inside, though, I was beaming.

Samuel drained his glass and picked up the bottle.

"Another, Alex?"

"Why not?" said the guest.

"Now, where's that butler when you need him?" said Samuel.

This is my chance, I thought.

"He's upstairs, sir," I said quickly. "Shall I get it for you?"

"Very good," said Samuel. "Save Lock's poor old knees on the cellar steps. I swear I can hear his joints over the gears of the omnibus."

Alexander laughed along with him, and I hurried out of the room. My heart was fluttering as I skipped down the steps to the scullery. Cook had her head up close to the open oven door, cleaning, and Rob was rubbing a piece of horse tack with a grubby cloth. "Everything dandy up there?" he said.

"Yes," I said. "They want another bottle."

Rob sighed. "They'll be drunk later."

Cook stopped her scrubbing for a moment, and Rob and I shared a look. Then she carried on.

"Need a hand with the hatch?" Rob asked.

I thanked him, and he hauled up the trapdoor easily. I descended the steps and went first to the spot behind the crates. I felt in the gloom and pulled out the Ouija cloth, then stuffed it in my apron. The wine rack was across the other side. I plucked out a bottle.

It was as easy as that.

Twenty-eight

SAMUEL AND ALEXANDER FINISHED THE SECOND
bottle more quickly than the first, and then retired to the
drawing room. I helped to wash the dishes, and Rowena
wound round my legs. The poor thing seemed lost now.
"Don't worry," I said. "I'll get her back."

I was getting ready to go to bed myself when I
remembered that I needed some sort of ball. What had
Dr. Reinhardt called it? A "pointer"? But what could I
use?

It came to me. In the drawing room was bowl of
carved and painted fruits. One of the tangerines would
do very well, and it was unlikely to be missed. However,
from the sounds spilling out into the main hallway it
seemed Alexander and Samuel would be ensconced
there for some time. They'd moved on to brandy or
whiskey, no doubt. I hesitated, trying to think up some

valid excuse to go in. Then footsteps came from the drawing room.

"Oh, Abi," said Samuel. He was a little red in the face and his words were slurred. I reflected that it was a good thing that Mrs. Cotton had gone to bed. No doubt she would have had something disapproving to say about his condition. "Abi, you can help us. We need more light for the camera."

"More light?"

"Yes, bring all the lanterns and candles you can find to the drawing room. Do you mind?"

"Of course not," I said.

I knew nothing about photographic equipment and wondered why their experiments couldn't wait until the following morning, but I stopped myself. The Ouija was safely stored upstairs, and it couldn't hurt to spare a few more minutes for Samuel. I went into the sitting room, the library, and the dining room for the lamps, then down to the scullery to fetch more candles. When Cook heard what Samuel and Alexander were up to, she tutted and said, "They'll be burning the bloody house down, they will."

I took everything through to the drawing room on a tray. When I arrived the curtains hadn't been drawn and the window glass reflected the inside of the room almost as cleanly as a mirror. A vase had been taken from the table, and on it stood a strange object the like of which I'd never seen before. It looked partly like a piece of furniture and partly like a musical instrument. Resting on a hinged platform, it comprised two polished wooden blocks joined by something like the bellows of an accordion, made of wood too rather than cloth or leather. From the far end a brass cylinder protruded, capped with a thick glass lens. It was as big as a medium-sized dog. Beside it a tray of liquid, supported on a tripod, was heating up over a low oil flame, while Alexander was buffing a transparent plate. It was as though I was at the center of some scientific experiment.

Samuel took the lamps and candles and arranged them around the center of the room. By the time they were all lit, it was as bright as day.

"Perhaps you'd like to be our first sitter, Abi?" said Samuel, adjusting the position of a lamp. I thought that Alexander looked a little put out at the suggestion. As for me, I wanted to get upstairs to the Ouija cloth.

"I should be getting to bed," I said.

"Nonsense!" said Samuel. "It will only take a moment."

He pulled an upright chair across and placed it in

front of the brass tube, about six feet away. He patted it. "Take a seat, then."

"Will it hurt?" I asked.

This brought a snigger from Alexander, who shook his head. "Not a bit, my girl."

I perched on the seat and looked towards the camera lens. Alexander slid the plate into the back of the machine and leaned down beneath a hood to look through the other side.

"A bit low," he muttered. He wound a small handle on the side and the lens titled upwards. "That's better. Right, Miss Tamper. I need you to stay absolutely still for about thirty seconds. Can you manage that?"

"Yes, sir."

"Good." He reached forward for the cap over the lens. "Ready?"

I nodded.

"Here we go, then. Don't move."

He whipped up the shutter.

I held my breath, but could feel Samuel standing behind me breathing very slowly as we both looked into the lens for half a minute. There was no whirring motor or grinding gears. It seemed to me amazing that this box of wood and metal could take our image without appearing to do anything at all.

Master Ambrose repositioned the cap. "Right. Lights out, please."

Samuel stood up and went round extinguishing the lamps and candles. I wasn't sure quite what we were doing, but I helped anyway. Soon the room was in darkness, and I saw his friend working over the heated liquid.

"The likeness needs to be developed quickly in the dark," explained Samuel. "That way the image becomes fixed."

"We'll leave it to dry overnight," said Alexander. "Will your aunt mind if we pin it up in here?"

"She won't have to," said Samuel. "It's my father's house, not hers."

Afterwards, with the portrait hanging to dry in the darkened room, Alexander Ambrose took his leave. On the way out of the drawing room I took one of the fake tangerines from the bowl. It wasn't perfectly round, but it would have to do.

With the front door locked and bolted by Samuel himself, he paused on the stairs.

"Are you feeling all right, Abi?" he asked. "You

don't seem yourself."

You don't know the half of it, I thought. And if I told you, you wouldn't believe me.

"Is it my aunt?" he said.

I didn't know what to say. It was as though he was reading my thoughts.

"I heard her the other night. Something about a key? You can tell me, Abi."

"She thinks I stole it," I said.

"And you didn't?"

I shook my head.

"Listen," he said. "Soon things will change around here. My father, he's—well, I'm sure you know he's very ill." A look of pain crossed his face. "I don't mind telling you his affairs are in a mess. Things will be better, I promise."

He'd never struggled with his words in the past, but I caught his meaning, or thought I did. Was he speaking of Mrs. Cotton? Was he saying she'd be out of our lives for good?

I didn't press him, and wished him goodnight.

Normally I would have fallen into bed after such a long day, but that night was different.

Outside my bedroom the wind was howling and buffeting the roof, and the old timbers creaked a little under the barrage. Rain lashed the window like volleys of pebbles thrown against the glass.

I unrolled the cloth on the floor by the light of a candle, and sat cross-legged beside it. It was freezing up there, but as I shivered in my thin nightdress, something warmed me inside. I remembered what Dr. Reinhardt had said about the spirit world – "pockets of oil and water." Perhaps one such pocket was forming around me now.

On the grey cloth the letters were unevenly sized and clumsily stitched, as if by a child learning her way with a needle and thread. Twenty-six letters around the outside, and the words "Aye" and "No." I wondered where it had come from—some gypsy market maybe. I wondered if it could really work.

I took out the wooden tangerine and placed it in the center of the cloth. If it hadn't been for all the other happenings in the house over the preceding days, I would have felt foolish. But now the room took on an extra dimension of coldness. The shadows deepened into purest black, and the cloth seemed almost to glow on the floor.

I did as Dr. Reinhardt had instructed and placed my fingers lightly over the top of the wooden orb, closing my eyes.

"Mama?" I whispered. "Is that you?"

Almost at once I felt a warmth in my fingertips, blood pulsing along my arms and through the pointer. It wasn't painful, but it was unsettling.

The ball started to move.

I've heard of such things since, of course, when a group of people gather in some deserted place—a graveyard or abandoned house. They stand in a ring around their board, placing their hands as one on some marker in the center. Inevitably, the pointer moves as it did for me that night. I'm skeptical, to be honest—in any group there will be a joker, someone who wants to frighten and be frightened.

But there was no one in that room with me. No person anyway.

The ball moved, and my fingers followed it.

When I dared to open my eyes, I saw that it rested over the word "Aye."

Another time I might have been afraid. But now I smiled as my eyes filled with tears.

The ball rocked under my fingers. Relief flooded through me and I cried with joy.

"Mama," I said, "were you poisoned?"

I closed my eyes again, and felt the ball roll.

Again it settled on "Aye."

I tried to control my breathing. I was sure I hadn't made it move. Absolutely sure.

I brought the ball back to the center of the cloth. There was only one more question I needed to ask. "Mama, was it Mrs. Cotton?"

The ball didn't move straight away, but slowly rolled to "No."

"What?" I said aloud. There must be some mistake.

I asked the same question again. "Was it Mrs. Cotton?"

This time the ball moved more steadily and directly. "No."

Not her? Then who? Suddenly I felt a flush of anger. What had Dr. Reinhardt sold me? I'd give up my father's watch for a worthless piece of junk. It didn't even work.

Or perhaps the spirit was confused. The doctor had said that too, hadn't he?

I asked a final time, enunciating each word clearly with my eyes tightly shut. "Did Mrs. Cotton poison you?"

Suddenly the ball was snatched away. I opened my eyes and saw that I was alone. The ball rattled across the floor and rolled to a halt by the window.

I didn't understand. Dr. Reinhardt hadn't mentioned

anything like this happening. Perhaps I'd caused it in my overexcitement.

I stood up and went to retrieve the wooden globe.

At the window, I heard something that sounded like the whisper of leaves. A fraction of a second later, I realized there were no leaves on the trees at this time of year.

I blew out the candle to see better and pressed my nose against the glass.

Outside it was very dark, and the thick clouds were deep and forbidding grey smudges. None of the houses beyond seemed to have their lights on, and their windows looked like a hundred black eyes peering back.

The lane beside the house was quiet, but not completely so. There was a movement—a figure slinking through the darkness against the wall opposite. I was struck immediately by the impression that he—for it was a man, I was sure—was up to no good. I strained my neck to watch him. Then he turned across the lane and I realized he was coming towards the back gate.

Towards the house.

Twenty-nine

I QUICKLY LEFT MY WINDOW AND HURRIED OUT of my room and down the stairs, still in my nightdress. A draft snaked around my ankles as I turned back along the corridor to the spare bedroom where I had left Rowena and her kittens. In there was a window that looked out into the stable yard.

He was over the gate when I saw him, and moving through the yard to the rear stable. He reached up through the hatch and took something from high up inside.

When he turned round again, I froze. He was looking up at the house as though he could see me, but I knew I must be wrong. There was no light behind me. He headed back towards the rear door, then took the steps up into the garden and towards the library.

He had the missing key.

My mouth was dry and I swallowed uncomfortably. What on earth could I do? I didn't dare wake Lizzy. Heaven knows what she'd have said. Nor Samuel— with only one leg to rely on, he would be in more danger than me. As for rousing Mrs. Cotton, that was unthinkable. Any alarm and the intruder would surely run, and what then? Would they even believe me?

But Rob would be sleeping, as he always did, in the china closet adjacent to the sitting room. He was brave and able-bodied. If I could get to him . . .

There was no time to waste. As I passed the main landing, I saw a candlestick on the table. I broke off the half-melted candle and hefted the silver. It was heavy enough to do some damage, if I dared to use it. I took the main stairs rather than the servants' ones, thinking that whoever had come in would be more likely to run if he thought a member of the household had awoken. When I reached the bottom, I stopped with my hand on the banister and listened.

There was no sound. I stepped down into the main hall. Maybe the man hadn't come in at all. Perhaps he'd turned at the back door and walked away, deciding that it was too great a risk.

Through the arch, I saw the library door was open. I remembered clearly that when I said goodnight to

Samuel, it had been closed. Mrs. Cotton insisted on all doors being shut when the house went to bed.

A rattle came from the dining room.

I looked across the hall to the sitting-room door. Rob was asleep in there. If I could just shout to him, he was sure to hear me. Something made me stop. Perhaps it was the years of being told never to raise my voice in the house, or simply the waves of blood pumping in my veins. If the intruder was in the dining room, all I needed to do was to close the door behind him and wedge a chair beneath the handle. Short of breaking a window and climbing out, he'd be trapped.

Then I could awaken the house.

I scurried on tiptoe towards the drawing room door. It was open. He had been in there too.

What was to be had, I wondered, but a few candle-sticks and the odd painting? I crept inside, found a chair and lifted it carefully. But something was wrong. With a mighty crash, something slid off the chair.

My feet were suddenly wet. The tray that had held the developing fluid was upturned on the floor.

A scrabbling followed and a man appeared at the doorway. He wore a cap pulled down low and a scarf fastened around the lower half of his face. His eyes, wide with shock, met mine.

My bowels threatened to give way, but he simply ran for the drawing-room door and back out into the hall.

Finally I screamed, first barely more than a whimper, then more loudly, piercing the silence. I grabbed up the candlestick and ran after him into the library. He was running for the French windows. I couldn't catch him, so I did the only thing I could think of.

I threw the candlestick.

Now, I wasn't what you'd call muscular, but the hours of scrubbing on my hands and knees had given me grit and a wiry strength. With a glint of flashing silver, the candlestick spun through the air and caught him with a soft thud on the back of the neck. He gave a cry, stumbled, and tripped over a library step. Without thinking, I picked up the candlestick and clubbed him again as he tried to rise. Groaning, he crawled on his hands and knees towards the library door. He reached up for the handle, but as he did so, I gripped his foot and pulled him back.

He rolled on to his back and let fly with a vicious kick. It caught me on the shoulder and I was thrown against the small sofa.

He was up again, and I could only watched dazed from the floor. He picked up the candlestick and advanced. I was afraid, of course, but I felt stupid too.

I shouldn't have come down, and now he was going to kill me. He lifted the candlestick.

Then his gaze shifted to something behind me.

"You'll put that down, lad!" said a voice.

I looked back from the floor, hardly believing my eyes. Rob stood there at the door in his nightshirt. I could have jumped up and kissed him.

Bless you, Robert Willmett!

The man with the candlestick bristled as though ready to fight, but then thought better of it. He dropped the weapon with a thunk on to the carpet and looked at me.

"Elizabeth said you was a sharp one," he said.

I recognized his voice straight away. He pulled off the scarf and I saw I was right.

It was Henry.

He didn't put up much of a fight but sat himself heavily on the library step. Gradually the house came alive around us: Mrs. Cotton, dark smudges under her eyes and a nightcap on her head; Mr. Lock looking like a corpse dug up and made to stand; Samuel struggling with his crutch. Only Lord Greave didn't appear. A constable was summoned and Cook brewed tea for everyone.

Lizzy was the last person to come down, and when

she did she gave a sad little groan. "Oh, Henry!" she said, seeming to take it all in without being told. "Why?"

I saw Mrs. Cotton twitch her nose, as though alert to all the possibilities that Lizzy's words offered. Her eyes narrowed. There was maybe a sliver of a chance that she wouldn't catch on, but then Henry mumbled, "Sorry, sweetheart," and buried his head in his hands. Mrs. Cotton lifted her chin. She knew now, for sure.

The constable, a man called Evans, asked Samuel what had happened. He in turn gestured to me, and in halting sentences I explained that I had heard a noise and described all that followed. I didn't mention that I'd been engaged in diabolical practices upstairs.

"Caught red-handed, it seems," said the constable. Henry didn't look up.

"Good work, Abi," said Samuel. "If it weren't for you, this miscreant might have got away."

I could hardly celebrate. The adrenaline had long since seeped away, leaving me cold and aching. Henry's arrest could only bring Lizzy more pain.

"And he got in through here, did he?" said the constable, walking towards the door. "Oh, what's this? He pulled the key from the outside lock. "Burglaries will happen if you leave the key in the lock."

Mrs. Cotton strode forward and snatched it from

the policeman's hand. "How dare you, sir!" she said. "Someone gave him this key, and I think I have a good idea who it was."

She glared at Lizzy, and I felt so sorry for her. The blood drained from her face as I watched, and she wobbled on her feet. Rob managed to get to her side before she fainted.

"Lay her in the sitting room," said Sammy, rubbing his temples in confusion. He turned to the constable. "Perhaps we could talk again in the morning, when everything is more clear."

Constable Evans nodded gravely. "I think that would be best for everyone, sir. In the meantime, I'll take this young man to a cell for the night. His employers are sure to want a word too."

He laid a strong hand on Henry's arm and led him along the hall.

As they were shown out I wandered through to the sitting room, where Lizzy was sitting up on the chaise lounge, sipping tea with a trembling hand. Her eyes were vacant though, and she seemed to be looking straight through me. It was as if all that had happened in the nursery was no longer important, or even remembered.

"How could he?" she said quietly. "I gave him that key for us. So he could come and see me last week. He must have had it copied."

I put my arms round her, and felt her stiffen.

"You'd better get to bed, Abigail," said Mrs. Cotton behind me.

I let go of Lizzy and stood up. Rob looked on uncertainly.

"Elizabeth and I need a moment to talk," the housekeeper said to him. "Perhaps you could make sure everything is put back straight in the other rooms."

Rob left without a word and I went after him, though I hated to do it. As I closed the door, I took a last look back into the room. Mrs. Cotton was standing over the prone Elizabeth like a doctor looking down at the body of one near death. Lizzy's lips were trembling, and I knew she was thinking not of Henry, or ghosts, or madness. She was thinking about the baby growing inside her.

Thirty

I DIDN'T HAVE THE ENERGY TO GO BACK TO THE
Ouija cloth that night. It was as if the spell had been
broken. I rolled it up and placed it beneath my pillow,
then lay in my bed and listened for Lizzy coming up the
stairs. She never did. Instead, some half an hour after
I'd left her, it was Mrs. Cotton's steps I heard. I braced
myself, thinking that she was going to burst through
my door. But she went into Lizzy's room for less than a
minute and then came out again without disturbing me.

Next morning I checked Lizzy's room, but saw that
the bed sheets were undisturbed. It was with a sense of
rising panic that I took the stairs down to the scullery.
Rowena rubbed against my legs, so I tickled her beneath
the chin. She looked perkier today, as if she'd almost

forgotten about her little ones. If only we could all move on so easily, I thought to myself.

Cook was seated on a stool near the hearth, gently crying. My first thought was that she'd been at the bottle already.

"What is it?" I asked.

She turned her face towards me. "Oh, Abi," she said. "She's gone!"

"Who? Lizzy?"

Cook nodded and blew her nose into a handkerchief.

"Sent away," she said. "Mrs. Cotton said she wasn't having her under her roof no longer."

It was worse than I'd expected. Far worse.

"But where's she gone?" I said. "She has nowhere but her sister's."

Cook said she didn't know, but that Lizzy had been dismissed by the back door the night before without any ceremony. She'd been given her belongings in a sack and thrust out into the cold.

"Like a pauper from the workhouse," Cook snivelled. "Just like little Anne."

I went to put my arm around her. What could I possibly do? As she shook with sobbing, my own tears remained inside. Anger burned. Mrs. Cotton doesn't have the right, I told myself. Lizzy made a stupid mistake trusting Henry, and she'd have to pay for that her whole life, but to throw her out was just too awful. It was the behavior of a heartless monster.

I made up my mind then and there what I would do. First I'd talk to Mrs. Cotton directly—try to reason with her. And if that didn't work—well, I'd go to Samuel. Mrs. Cotton might not like it—it might offend her sense of what was right—but I'd have given her a chance. Sammy would understand. He'd see what was fair and overrule his aunt, as it was his right to do. He'd send Rob over to Lizzy's sister's lodgings, or maybe he'd even go himself. By nightfall, Lizzy would be back in Greave Hall.

"There are fires to be lit," said Mrs. Cotton.

She stood in the doorway opposite, having come down the main stairs. She was dressed in a tight-fitting black dress with black lace collar, and her hair was pulled back in an even tighter bun than normal. Her hands were clasped in front of her.

"May I speak to you?" I said as firmly as I could.

Her eyebrows twitched. "You may, Miss Tamper. Come over here and say your piece."

She walked into the servants' hallway and I followed. She stood at the bottom of the stairs with her back half-turned to me. It was disconcerting not being able to see her face, but I pressed my case.

"Elizabeth should be given a second chance," I said. "She was duped by that charlatan. She never would have—"

"What is the eighth commandment?" Mrs. Cotton interrupted.

I thought for a moment. I didn't really care for Bible learning, but I wasn't a simpleton. "Thou shalt not steal," I said.

"And she stole from me," said the housekeeper. She began to walk up the stairs as though the conversation was over, so I went after her. She turned on me in disgust.

"What do you think you're doing?" she said. "Get off these stairs at once!"

I held my ground. "Lizzy doesn't deserve it."

Mrs. Cotton spoke again, her voice more threatening. "I decide what the staff of this house deserve," she said. "Elizabeth let us all down, and that is why she can't ever come back."

"But she has nothing else," I said. Surely that simple fact would touch Mrs. Cotton somewhere.

"She was lost long before now," said Mrs. Cotton with a smile. "Don't think I'm stupid, Miss Tamper. I know exactly what goes on under this roof."

From her sly look, I guessed she must mean Lizzy's condition.

"Then it's two lives you're destroying," I said quietly.

In times past that would have merited a thrashing and a half, but now she simply turned away and continued up the stairs.

I went about my work, if not with zeal, then with a determination I hadn't felt for a long time. By nine, Samuel still hadn't stirred. I was hardly surprised after the events of the night before. As soon as he was up, I planned to speak to him. It was laundry day, so I went from room to room gathering the sheets and other washing. Lord Greave, seemingly oblivious to what had happened the night before, took a few turns round the garden in his robe and slippers. I watched him from the back door. His hands were moving as though he was giving a speech and he was muttering to himself. Perhaps Sammy was right—perhaps something would need to be done about him too.

Samuel must have gone out while I was washing pillowcases in soapy water, because the wheelchair that had been parked in the hallway was gone. I guessed that Rob was taking him for some fresh air. I wondered if either of them knew yet about Lizzy's disappearance. Rob was the type who might not even mention it if he did. At about eleven o'clock the front doorbell rang. Normally Lizzy herself would have gone for it, or else Mr. Lock, but the butler had taken His Lordship upstairs to dress. I quickly dried my hands and rushed upstairs.

I reached the door at the same time as Mrs. Cotton. As she opened it, we both got a nasty surprise. Standing there on the step was Dr. Reinhardt.

My throat went dry. Had Mrs. Cotton summoned him again? Would he betray me in front of her? We'd hardly parted on good terms, so there was no reason why he should keep our meeting a secret.

"Doctor?" said Mrs. Cotton. The bemusement in her tone told me straight away that she wasn't expecting this visit. I started to back away, fear making me feel sick. If I could hide somewhere, perhaps he wouldn't see me.

"And Constable Evans," said Mrs. Cotton. "How strange to see you again so soon."

I was confused. Did this have something to do with Henry and the foiled burglary? But how was Dr. Reinhardt involved in all that?

"Mrs. Cotton," said the constable. "Sorry to bother you on what I'm sure is a busy day. We need to speak to a member of your staff, if that's possible."

My heart sank. I still wasn't sure what was going on, but the uneasy feeling was spreading into my legs, making my knees weak.

"Oh, yes?" said the housekeeper. "And who might that be?"

"The serving girl," said Dr. Reinhardt. "Miss Tamper."

Thirty-one

MRS. COTTON EYED ME WARILY AS WE ASSEMBLED in the sitting room. She looked as confused as I was. Dr. Reinhardt and Mrs. Cotton sat on opposite sofas, while the constable remained standing. I was perched on a high-backed chair. As we were settling Mr. Lock came in as well, shutting the door behind him.

"Is there some sort of problem?" he asked.

"Possibly," said the constable. "We're carrying out some enquiries into a burglary carried out some years ago. Dr. Reinhardt has been very helpful, but we still have a loose end your girl here might be able to tie up." The constable fished in his pocket for a moment, then brought out a silver object—my father's watch. The hands were still motionless, I noticed. "Do you recognize this?" he said to me.

I couldn't find my words. Whatever I said now, I was

trapped good and proper. There seemed little chance that I could leave this room without Mrs. Cotton learning of my night-time excursion. I thought the best thing was to tell the truth, but not to give away information if not specifically asked.

"Well?" he said.

"It's her watch," said Mr. Lock helpfully.

"My father's watch," I clarified.

"Your father's, you say?" said the constable. "And that'll be Jim Tamper, I presume?"

I frowned. How did this policeman know of my father? "James Tamper, sir."

Mrs. Cotton was wearing a look of absolute concentration. I could almost hear the cogs in her mind turning, trying to make sense of what was going on in front of her eyes.

"And he gave it to you?" said the constable.

"He gave it to my mother, sir," I said. "And she gave it me. She's passed on too."

"You believe your father is dead?" said the constable.

He spoke with some surprise and the words sank in. I replied hesitantly. "He is, sir," I said. "Died before I was even born."

"She said the same to me," said Dr. Reinhardt.

Mr. Lock coughed uncomfortably in the corner of the

room, but held up a hand to apologize.

I was replaying the constable's strange words in my head: *You believe your father is dead.*

"This watch is stolen property," said the constable. "It was taken in a substantial heist on Frobisher's Jewelers on Bond Street several years ago. The culprit was never identified and most of the pieces were lost."

The words washed over me. I didn't just believe my father was dead, I knew it. My mother wouldn't have lied to me.

"Excuse me," said Mrs. Cotton. "How did this watch come to be in your possession, constable?"

Her question shook me from my thoughts. She had to find out now.

"This gentleman tried to pawn the watch two days ago," said the policeman, gesturing to Dr. Reinhardt. "The owner of the shop notified us, and we followed the trail back here."

Mrs. Cotton's frown deepened and her nostrils flared slightly, like a creature responding to the sudden scent of prey close by.

"But how did this gentleman get his hands on it?" she asked impatiently.

Finally Dr. Reinhardt spoke. "She had no money to pay for my services. We agreed the watch was a suitable remuneration."

That was it, then. Any chance I had of squeezing out of this was gone.

But Mrs. Cotton didn't pursue it further. The only thing I could think was that she had something worse planned for me. Mr. Lock seemed to be squirming slightly in the corner.

"Perhaps we should conclude the matter then," said the butler. "It seems that we'll never know how the watch came to be in Abigail's possession, but at least it can be returned to its rightful owner." He held open the door, as if to suggest it was time the guests left.

I found my voice to ask the question that everyone seemed to have forgotten.

"Wait a moment," I said. "My father is dead, isn't he?"

Dr. Reinhardt raised his eyebrows and Mr. Lock laughed uncomfortably. Mrs. Cotton remained impassive.

The constable looked from one to the other, then sat down beside me. "Jim Tamper was transported after the Henley Thefts in '38."

"Transported?" I said.

"That's right. Sent to Australia," said the constable. "We never could pin the Frobisher job on him, but it seems this is the missing piece of the puzzle."

"No," I said. "My father was apprenticed to a watchmaker."

The constable smiled as if I was a stupid toddler. "Looks like someone's been telling you some porky pies, my girl. Tamper was a swindler if ever I saw one. He'll still be breaking rocks now, I expect."

"It's a lie," I said. "My mother—"

"Told you what she thought was best, I expect," he said. "Sorry you have to find out the truth from me."

But something else was troubling me. I couldn't put my finger on exactly what.

"What were the Henley thefts?" I asked.

Mrs. Cotton seemed to growl, but she didn't interrupt. I think she was as interested as me.

"First regatta on the river there," said Constable Evans. "Jim Tamper sneaked up through the kitchens of the Red Lion hotel, ransacked all the rooms, and tried to make his getaway by boat. It was only a servant like yourself spotted him."

I realized what it was that troubled me.

"You said this was 1838, though. Are you sure?"

"I think we've used enough of the constable's time," said Mr. Lock. "Gentlemen, I'll see you out."

"Oh, quite sure," said the constable. "Not every day you hear of a chase by boat, is it?"

Lock finally succeeded in showing Constable and Dr. Reinhardt out of the door and Mrs. Cotton left me on my own. It couldn't be true. There had to be some mistake. My father couldn't have been arrested in 1838 for one very good reason: I wasn't born until February 1840. Either the constable's memory was at fault, or there was only one other conclusion.

James Tamper wasn't my father.

Thirty-two

As soon as the thought lodged in my mind, I couldn't dismiss it. I think I knew straight away that it was true. Why else had my mother hardly ever spoken of my father? Why hadn't she visited his grave? And, strangely, even Dr. Reinhardt had assumed he was alive. For some reason, after all that had happened it was the doctor's words I trusted most of all.

I suddenly felt very sad—not just for myself, and the shadow of a father who had now vanished, but for my poor mother too. To be married to a rascal like that, and to be left alone! No wonder she had gone into service for Eleanor Greave. Without a husband to support her, she must have been desperate for money.

I could barely think of what must have happened. Had my mother made the same mistake as Lizzy, falling for a follower and then being deserted? She seemed so level-headed, so sensible. How it must have angered Mrs. Cotton that my mother—a mere member of staff—was allowed to stay on with the disgrace of a fatherless child. How it must have maddened her to see me grow up in the house that she thought hers by right through her dead sister. The fury must have ripened and fermented over the years, until one day she had snapped and taken her revenge.

I stood up, and found my hands were balled into fists. I made up my mind then to tell Samuel as soon as he got back. Until then I would avoid Mrs. Cotton as well as I could. She had not reappeared to question me further about Dr. Reinhardt, and I knew why. It was guilt. She might not know it for sure, but she at least suspected that I was on to her. She dared not challenge me for fear that I would tell everyone her secret.

Well, I shall, I promised myself. And that will be the end of you.

On my way back down to the laundry, I heard muffled voices from the library. I pressed my ear against the door. It was Mrs. Cotton talking. Her tone was barely a hiss, and I could tell immediately that I was the subject being discussed.

"She must not know," said Mrs. Cotton.

"But . . ." it was Mr. Lock, his voice plaintive. "His Lordship—"

"My brother-in-law doesn't know whether it's day or night," she snapped. "Just burn them! Or I will."

I heard them moving towards the door and quickly darted along the corridor and into the drawing room. Mrs. Cotton emerged first and strode towards the servants' stairs. Mr. Lock came more slowly behind, his sagging shoulders seeming to bear an extra weight. He had been asked to do something of which he didn't approve—something involving me.

As he went to the main stairs, I went to the back ones.

He continued past the first floor, slowly approaching Lord Greave's chamber. Now things were awkward. If I were caught here, there'd be trouble. I planned an excuse that I was coming to check what clean bed linen was needed. It wasn't convincing, but neither was it ridiculous.

As soon as he rounded the corner to Lord Greave's room, I trod lightly after him. I hovered at the end of the corridor leading to Lord Greave's private rooms. I could hear Mr. Lock breathing heavily.

I crept along the corridor after him.

I had to know.

At the door, I peered in. He was bent over, rifling through the contents of Lord Greave's little desk. He pulled out a sheaf of documents secured with a piece of string, untied them quickly and leafed through them, removing a few sheets of paper, then disappeared from my line of sight towards the other side of the room.

Towards the fire.

I looked farther in. Sure enough, he was crouched beside the grate and feeding the pieces of paper into the small dying fire. I wanted nothing more than to stop him, to run in and tear them out, but it was unthinkable to go in there without permission.

So, hating myself every step of the way, I retreated back down the main stairs. Whatever was in those documents, I would never know.

A cry came from the bedroom—a howl of terror. I quickly scampered out of the way to the back stairs as Mr. Lock shuffled into sight. His eyes were wide with fear, his skin pale. He didn't see me as he half-fell, half-stumbled down the steps, supporting himself with the banister. He looked like he'd had a terrible fright.

He ran past as rapidly as his old legs would carry him, and down the next stairs to the ground floor. I realized this would be my only chance, and sprinted back up along the corridor and into His Lordship's room. In the grate, the papers were blazing. A wail escaped my lips when I saw that most were already in ashes. I grabbed the poker and pushed them out of the fire. A fringe of orange was creeping across the pages, so I picked up an edge and blew out the flames, shaking the embers off. I ran quickly back to the door and down the stairs, clutching the papers to my stomach.

What was written on them, I couldn't know. Something important enough to burn. Something to do with me.

I couldn't help feeling that I was holding my past in my hands.

Back in my room I examined the papers carefully. It was a letter—two sheets, written in uneven lines. Both had been mostly eaten away or blackened by the fire, so only a little of the writing was left at the top of the pages, but it was addressed to "Darling Nathan, my love." Nathan? His Lordship's first name was Nathaniel. This was his private correspondence. A love letter? I knew that I should stop reading there and then.

The letter had a date at the top: "the third of August. On the second page, only a few lines remained. The signature caught my eye at once.

"All my love, Susan."

I'm not sure how long I sat there, but it was until my backside was numb and long after. My mother had been in love with Lord Greave! I felt like a ship unmoored and floating over a misty lake, the banks nowhere in sight.

I suppose I knew what the letter would say before I started reading, but read it I did, many times over. What came across most strongly was my mother's voice: kind, loving, a hint of a smile even when what she spoke of was serious.

> *Little Sammy is sure to pick up on it; you would be surprised how perceptive youngsters can be. I thought today that Trevor had seen us share a kiss on the stairs.*
>
> *We must be more careful from now on, Nathan. Do not despair though. With our secret way—*

A patch was burnt from the middle of the letter and only a few more sentences remained.

> *I don't expect any of them will understand, least of all Lillian. You say you are happy for all to know. Well, I am not, and I expressly forbid it. For a man of your—*

Then just a fraction more:

> *You scoff at appearances, but they are everything. What matters is our love. Our child. Nothing more—*

"Our child."

Me.

The product of an affair between the master and the servant, the celebrated naval lord and his son's nurse. Had they really thought it was easier for me to grow up thinking my father was dead? I felt a sadness, a deep ache in my heart that my mother and I had never shared the truth.

In a single day I had lost one father and found another. The dates fitted perfectly. She had learned that she was pregnant with me some time in June 1839.

"You could have told me before," I said aloud. Everything had to adjust, but it was like a jigsaw puzzle thrown into the air. I knew the pieces would somehow fit together again, but the picture would be different. I caught glimpses of it though, like a landscape illuminated under lightning.

Samuel, who'd always been like an older brother to me, was indeed my real half-brother. My mother had been happy all along; she'd found love again after James Tamper had left.

There were more bitter realizations as well and they led me on to a darker train of thought. Mrs. Cotton was actually my aunt. She had known her brother-in-law's secret all along. She feared that my mother would supplant her, that Lord Greave would elevate her within the household, that she, Lillian Cotton, would have to answer to the nursemaid.

Had she known from the start though, or was it the discovery of the affair that had driven her to murder? When had Mr. Lock—or Trevor, as my mother called him—found out? They both knew of the letters, but had been willing to let them gather dust in a drawer until now. As long as they were safely out of the way in the attic desk.

I felt like confronting them there and then, but I wasn't sure what good it would do. I'd seen with what a heavy heart Mr. Lock had carried out his duties. He'd done it to protect his master, not through any spite harbored in his own breast. No, I had only one enemy in this house and it seemed she would stop at nothing to keep me in my place.

I stacked the letters carefully and placed them in my chest. Now at least I had an advantage over her. I knew the secret that she'd tried her hardest to destroy.

I felt like my drifting boat had finally bumped against the shore.

Thirty-three

EVEN THE HOUSE SEEMED DIFFERENT. Finishing the laundry and cleaning the rooms, I noticed things I never had before: the beauty of the seascapes in the sitting room, the patches of wear on the chairs around the dining table, the fine carvings on the mantel in the library. The garden outside seemed to glow in the late afternoon winter light. It was as if I myself were a different person inhabiting the new space.

I saw Lord Greave only once, shuffling in through the front door before dinner. Suddenly even the thought of addressing him seemed an impossibility. But fate intervened.

When it was time to take up His Lordship's brandy, Mr. Lock refused point blank to go, claiming his legs were bad. I suspected the real reason was that he feared whatever he had encountered earlier that day. I was happy, though, to carry up the tray.

Lord Greave sat in his chair beside the window, with a blanket over his knees.

My father.

I placed his decanter and glass on the low table beside him, then went to stoke his fire, which was smoldering weakly. From the corner of my eye, I watched him, searching his face to see something of myself. We both had blue eyes and slightly upturned noses, but that was all.

Observing him discreetly, I realized there was more to His Lordship's silence than mere age. Now I fancied I could see deeper into his vacant sadness. There was loneliness too, wrapping itself around him like a shroud. I'd always dated his decline to the time when Samuel left for war, but now I saw it was not then at all. It dated from seventeen minutes past four, one day just over a year ago.

He was mourning for a woman whom he'd never been able to publicly acknowledge. There were no others to share his grief, so it was locked within him, carried on memories.

From the corner of my eye, beside the fireplace where the letters had almost been destroyed, I saw through the open door of his dressing room. Almost at once a phrase from the letters jumped into my mind and two pieces of the puzzle slotted together.

"Our secret way . . ."

I felt a flush of heat, and it wasn't from the coals. The handprint on the hatch. My mother's handprint. What else could the "secret way" have been, if not a way for them to see each other secretly without the rest of the house knowing? She must have used the hatch rather than the main stairs, where housekeeper or butler might have seen her.

As I stood up from the fire, trying to contain my excitement, Lord Greave spoke and his voice was bitter.

"Samuel used to bring me up my drink, you know," he said.

"Yes, sir," I said. "But he can't now."

I wondered if he'd already forgotten about Sammy's leg.

He looked out of the window again. I filled his glass and placed it in front of him. He didn't even acknowledge me.

It's too late for us, I thought. I could see that now. He might have been a father to me once, but that time had passed.

"Will there be anything else, sir?" I asked.

He continued to look out of the window.

"Thank you, Abigail," he said.

It was the first time he'd used my name in a year.

I slept soundly that night until a dream shook me awake.

I was drifting high above the park on a cushion of warm cloud, approaching Greave Hall. All the windows were open as though the house was being aired, but I couldn't see any people until I came closer. Then I made out Lizzy in her window, high on the side of the house. She waved to me happily, and I felt so glad that she was back home.

I saw a dark shape behind her in the room. From its outline, I knew it was Mrs. Cotton. She was approaching stealthily, and Lizzy had no idea she was there. I shouted and shouted until my voice was hoarse, but the sound didn't carry. I knew for a certainty that the housekeeper meant to push Elizabeth out, and she would fall three floors to her death.

But there was nothing I could do. I was too far away. Mrs. Cotton's eyes glinted like a cat's in the moonlight.

I woke breathing heavily.

I washed and dressed carefully. Today was going to be a very special day and I wanted to look my best.

After breakfast, I found Samuel in the sitting room reading *The Times*. He was smartly dressed in a grey suit with waistcoat. Even with the trouser leg stitched up beneath his right knee, he looked every inch the gentleman around town.

"Hello, Abi," he said.

"Morning, Sammy," I said. "You going out today?"

He shook his head. "No, I have some appointments here actually."

I paused at the door, trying to find the right words to begin. But I was tongue-tied.

It was now or never.

"Sammy, do you remember ever meeting my father?"

He hardly looked up from his newspaper.

"Hmm, I don't think he ever came here, did he? I must have been, what, three or four when he died."

"He's not dead," I said.

Samuel looked up properly now and lowered the pages.

"Say again?"

"My father isn't dead," I said. "My father wasn't called Tamper at all."

He put down the newspaper carefully and stood up. Leaning on his single crutch, he crossed the room slowly to the window, and looked out towards the Park. It wasn't the reaction I expected. "Sammy?" I said, walking a few steps closer, then hesitating once more. The words were there now, waiting in my throat. They emerged in a whisper. "My father is Lord Greave."

Samuel didn't move for several seconds, and I heard the ticking of the clock in the hall. I could never have guessed what he would say next. He sighed heavily and nodded his head a fraction, still facing away from me.

"So now you know."

Thirty-four

AT FIRST I THOUGHT I MUST HAVE MISHEARD.
"You knew?"

He turned slowly from the window. "I suspected."

My breath was coming in gasps as I struggled to understand what he was telling me. "But—but why did you never say?"

Sammy watched me with large, sad eyes. "I didn't know for sure. I could hardly ask my father, and I didn't want to upset you without first knowing that I was right. What a mess families are, eh, Abi?"

He was smiling now, and held out his arms to me. I walked across the room and fell into them, hugging him tightly. "Shall I call you my little sister?" he said, laughing.

I realized I was crying. Never in my dreams had I imagined he would be so—well, so easy about it. I knew he'd always cared for me, of course, but this was too, too good of him.

"You can call me what you wish," I said through the tears. "Oh, I've wet your clothes."

He held me at arm's length and looked down at me. "Well, little sister, how did you find out?"

"I found a letter, half-burned in the grate. It was from my mother to your father. Here . . ." I fished the pages out of my apron and handed them to him.

He read them closely. I don't know what made me tell a white lie. I suppose there was so much to say, I didn't want to rush things.

"I know I shouldn't have looked," I said, "but I saw her name and, well . . ."

"I understand," he said, nodding. He put the letters down on the window sill. "And have you told my—our father?"

I shook my head. "I saw him last night, when I took his drink up. I'm afraid he—he was—"

"Mad?" said Samuel matter-of-factly. "There's no need to skirt around it, Abi. The man's lost his mind." He grimaced. "If only I'd been here more, perhaps we could have helped him together."

"We can help him now," I suggested.

"It's too late for that, I fear," said Samuel. "He

can't look after himself any more—barely eats a thing. The only thing we can do for him now is make him comfortable, take away the few remaining stresses in his life. In fact I've got Dr. Ingle coming to take a look. See if there's some specialist help we can get for him."

I thought how brave Sammy was then, taking on such responsibility. It must have been so hard to watch his father slip away like that. He dragged my attention back to more pressing matters. "I take it you haven't told anyone else yet?" he said, sounding tired now. He cocked his head. "Elizabeth, maybe?"

"No," I said. "Haven't you heard? Mrs. Cotton sacked Lizzy. Sent her away because of the burglary."

"My aunt is very strict," he replied.

"But it wasn't Lizzy's fault," I said. "Sammy, you can talk to her. Make her see sense."

Samuel frowned. "From what I understand, she gave this chap a key so he could sneak in and see her after hours. Sounds like a sackable offence to me."

"Please, Sammy," I said. "She's my friend. Do it for me."

His frown lifted and he sighed. "For you then, Sister," he said. "But you must do something for me."

"What's that?" I said.

He tapped the side of his nose. "Keep all this

between us for now, will you? Just till we have the arrangements with Father sorted out. I don't want to upset him more than necessary."

"Of course," I said. We hugged again. "I'd better be getting back to work now."

"For the time being, that's wise," he said. "Of course after the big announcement, all that will change. Can't have the daughter of the house scrubbing pans, can we?"

I laughed, feeling a tingle of excitement. "Mrs. Cotton won't be happy," I said. "You know that, don't you?"

Samuel shrugged. "Is she ever?"

I didn't think he'd spoken to her at lunch, because when she went out shopping afterwards, she looked serious but not aggrieved. About an hour after she left, three gentlemen arrived. There was Alexander, carrying a package under one arm, Dr. Ingle Senior, and an older man with long grey whiskers and long white hair like a lion's mane. Samuel thanked them for coming and I took their coats. Mr. Lock was sent to bring down Lord Greave, and I to prepare tea for the guests. The arrival was the cause of some excitement below stairs.

"What's happening?" said Rob. "Who's the old duffer?"

I didn't let on that I knew anything at all, but even I was slightly intrigued as to who the "old duffer" might be.

I took up the china and beverages just as Mr. Lock was coming the other way from the sitting room. Samuel was leaning against the doorway, and though I didn't hear what he said I could see he had an imploring look on his face. Mr. Lock looked at me, shaking his head and muttering angrily. "I'll have nothing to do with it," he said. "Nothing at all."

I couldn't think what he meant, but Samuel gave me a sad smile and hobbled aside to let me pass. Lord Greave was sitting in the same place where I had sat for my interview with the constable, and the other men were arranged around the opposite side of the room.

"And can you remember your wife's name?" said Dr. Ingle.

"Of course I can," said Lord Greave. "Eleanor Anne."

The older man with the moustache huffed. "This is ridiculous," he said. "An insult to my client."

I was putting down the tray when Alexander said, "No insult is intended, I assure you, Mr. Carter. We only intend to ascertain whether His Lordship—"

"There's no need to speak as though I'm not in the room," said Lord Greave.

"Father," said Samuel, "would you mind leaving us for a moment?"

"So I'm no longer welcome in my own parlor!" said His Lordship.

"Please, Father."

"A waste of everybody's time!" said Mr. Carter.

"I'm inclined to agree," said Dr. Ingle.

Lord Greave looked quite serene, but stood up. "I shall be in my library, should you require my presence again. If not, good day, gentlemen."

He left the room and I followed, closing it behind me. As he went into the library, he turned to me.

"Silly, isn't it, Susan? They seem to think I've lost my marbles."

It still wasn't clear to me what was going on, but I found Mr. Lock sitting with Cook and Rob at the kitchen table. Their faces were grave.

"Have they finished with him?" asked Mr. Lock in disgust.

"I don't understand. They're asking him all sorts of odd questions," I said.

"They're wanting to send him away," said Cook

sadly. "To a madhouse."

I gasped. "I'm sure that's not true. Sam—Master Greave only wants what's best for His Lordship."

Rob snorted. "Master Greave wants this place for himself."

I leapt to his defense.

"You shouldn't speak of things you don't understand," I said angrily.

They all looked up at that. "I mean," I said, "that a son naturally wants his father to suffer as little as possible. You know that His Lordship isn't well—we all do. Especially Master Greave."

They didn't look convinced. I could hardly let them know what Samuel had told me—that he was trying to ease the burden on his father. They were so distrustful of goodness.

The gentlemen left shortly afterwards. At the door, Mr. Carter turned to Samuel and pointed a chubby finger. He didn't seem to care if I heard. "My firm has served your family for upwards of fifty years, young sir, and I hope the relationship will continue for fifty more, but I must say I have found today's meeting a plain waste of my time and yours."

I could see hurt in Samuel's eyes.

"Mr. Carter, I appreciate your coming at short

notice. You too, doctor. All I can say is that this display of lucidity is quite out of character. He's a different person normally, and barely leaves his rooms."

"Master Greave speaks the truth, gentlemen," cut in Alexander. "I have seen much of His Lordship over the past few weeks, and as a student of law myself—"

"A student, indeed!" said Mr. Carter. A spot of red had appeared on each of his cheeks. "Well, sir, I have been practicing for more years than you have been on this good earth, and if I was feeling less diplomatic than I am, I'd say this whole thing stinks." He nodded to Mr. Lock. "Please pass on my good wishes to His Lordship."

With that he climbed into his waiting carriage.

Thirty-five

DR. INGLE AND ALEXANDER LEFT AS WELL, AND Samuel retreated to the sitting room. He looked utterly defeated, sitting with his head buried in his hands. I went to him and rested my hand on his good leg.

"Is there anything I can do?" I asked.

"There's nothing anyone can do," he said. "I simply don't understand it."

"What did that man mean?" I asked. "That he'd served the family."

"That was Wallis Carter," said Samuel. "My father's solicitor. I was hoping that if I got them together, the doctors and the lawyers, then they would see my father would be better off elsewhere."

"You mean the—" I was going to say "madhouse," but that wasn't right, "You mean an asylum?"

Pain was etched on Samuel's face. "A hospital,"

said Samuel. "I want him to be looked after. By God, Lock can barely get up the stairs without clutching at his chest. Rob's heart's in the right place, but he can't give my father the necessary care . . ." He ran his hand through his hair again and looked at me with wretched eyes. "Abi, they think I want his money, for heaven's sake!"

I felt powerless. I could see both sides.

"Well, he seemed to be much better today," I offered. "He was very"—What was the word Alexander used?—"very lucid."

"But what about tomorrow?" said Samuel. "And the next day?" He was almost ranting now. "What about when he decides to thrust his hand in the fire because he's feeling cold, or steps under a carriage when his mind's elsewhere? Oh, Abi, I don't know that I could live with myself!"

He was distraught. "But I could look after him," I said. "Now that we know the truth. I'd be glad to, after all he did for my mother and me. And there's Mrs. Cotton, of course—"

"Lillian!" Samuel exploded. "Abi, I'd no more trust my aunt to saddle Lancelot than to look after my father. The first chance she got, she'd—" He broke off.

But I had caught his meaning, and wanted more.

"You think she means him harm?" I said.

"Forgive me, I've spoken out of turn."

"No," I said. "Go on, Sammy."

He leaned back on the sofa, and didn't speak for a long time.

"I shouldn't say this," he said, "but you're one of the family now; you need to know."

"Yes?" I said.

"I think that Lillian might have been taking advantage of my father, in his less lucid moments. I spoke to Lock, but the old chap was too damned reticent to say anything. I think she might be taking his money."

I nodded, ready to tell him about all the other things: the dinner parties while he'd been away, the borrowed clothes and jewelry from his mother, the beatings. I saw the conversation in my mind's eye, building to a crescendo—the accusation that I'd harbored since that first visit by Dr. Reinhardt. That she was a murderer.

At that moment the door opened, and a breath of cold air blew through the sitting room, bringing with it Mrs. Cotton. How long she'd been standing at the door, I didn't know.

"Do you not have work to do?" she said.

I glanced at Sammy, who looked suddenly anxious. He gave me a little nod, as if to say, "You should be on your way; now is not the time."

So I went past Mrs. Cotton and out of the door, without even a trace of the fear I used to feel. She could do nothing to me now.

Whether it was through contrivance or unlucky chance, Mrs. Cotton had kept me busy until late at night. I didn't have a chance to speak with Samuel about the most important matters. I lay in bed, wondering where Lizzy was now. I tried to think of her tucked up safely at her sister's house.

The next morning, after the fires were done in all the downstairs rooms, I went up to light His Lordship's. How would he be this morning? I wondered. Perhaps we could have a proper conversation. I felt the overwhelming urge to thank him for all he'd done. For loving my mother and taking her in. For looking after us both.

His room was dark as always, and I knelt beside the grate to get the kindling started beneath the coals.

It was then that I noticed his hand trailing from the side of the bed. My first impression was that such a posture must be very uncomfortable for him. Then I saw that his eyes were open. He was watching me silently. I stood up in sudden fright.

"Sir?" I said.

He didn't answer.

"Lord Greave?"

I realized then that he was dead.

Thirty-six

I RAN TO THE TOP OF THE STAIRS AND CALLED down. "Sammy! Sammy!" I shouted. Mrs. Cotton was first out of her room, with a look of confusion and rage.

"In the name of God, girl, what are you screaming about?"

"His Lordship—"

She gripped the banisters and made her way quickly past me. I was trembling where I stood as Samuel next emerged from his room in his dressing gown. His hair, normally so tidy, was flopping over his forehead.

"Sammy," I said. "Please, Sammy. Come up."

He must have understood, because he went back into his room to fetch his crutch.

"Help me, will you?" he said. I could see his face already creasing, as if tears were close to the surface.

I went down and took his left arm over my shoulder

and together we climbed the stairs. Mrs. Cotton was standing over the bed. She wasn't crying—in fact she showed no emotion at all.

"He's dead," she said.

Samuel shook his head, but his eyes were fixed on his father's body.

"But . . . but yesterday, he was fine. He was healthy. It can't—"

I had stopped shaking. I'd seen one other dead body before, and that was my own mother. But there was something about this picture of death that troubled me. I couldn't put my finger on it then.

"The doctor must be sent for," Mrs. Cotton said coldly.

Dr. Ingle came and went quickly, expressing his regrets to both son and housekeeper. Heart failure, he announced, according to Rob. At about eleven o'clock we staff were confined to the lower ground floor while the undertakers came to take away the body. We could hear them grunting with the exertions of getting it down all the flights of steps. Rob, red-eyed, stood up at one point and said desperately, "I should go and help them," but Mr. Lock insisted it was the family's business, not ours.

Shortly after, Rob found something to do when he was asked to prepare the carriage. Apparently Sammy would be going to see the funeral directors. He requested that Mr. Lock go with him. On his way out, the butler asked that I draw the curtains across the house, in mourning, then clean His Lordship's room. Sammy nodded his approval. "If you wouldn't mind, Abi," he said.

Rob helped him out to the waiting carriage.

I went to the cupboard on the first floor to get the polishes and brushes, then continued up to the room. The bed was unmade and the imprint of His Lordship's body was still clear on the sheets. The fire was burning as if the occupant was expected back at any moment.

I looked at the bed and had an odd sensation that something wasn't right. Then I saw it.

The pillows.

They lay side by side. One had been beneath His Lordship's head, the other was on the opposite side of the bed.

He never sleeps like that, I thought. He always sleeps with two pillows beneath his head.

Maybe he'd only just gone to bed, and collapsed while getting in. That would explain his arm, flung so awkwardly to one side.

Or else . . . I could hardly bear to think it.

Or else somebody had come into the room the previous night. They'd pulled one of the pillows from underneath His Lordship's head and held it over his face while he struggled to claw them off. Then they'd put the pillow to one side, not knowing how particular the dead man was about his habits.

First my mother and now my father.

My legs felt weak. Why hadn't I spoken to Samuel yesterday? With mounting horror, I recalled what he'd said—that his aunt might . . . do something if she had the chance. Well, now she'd done it. She'd smothered a weak old man in his bed.

As I went down the stairs, my resolve strengthened. I had stalled for long enough. I reached the kitchen breathless.

"Miss McMahon?" I called, searching the rooms for Cook. "Deirdre?"

She wasn't in the scullery or the kitchen. The water closet was unoccupied. I looked out of the back door, then went through into the laundry. Was she using the opportunity to take a drink somewhere? I wondered. I even checked the pantry. "Cook?"

"I sent her out," said Mrs. Cotton.

I spun round and pressed myself up against the pantry door.

She stood not four feet behind me, with her hands behind her back. She never stood like that normally, and I sensed she was holding something.

Fear took hold of my stomach and squeezed.

"Sent her where?" I said.

She didn't answer at first, but looked at me as if she could burn me with her eyes.

"On some errands," she said.

I flicked a glance to my left. The door to the servants' hall was closed. I could get to it before her, but she'd reach me before I could escape.

There was a rolling pin on the sideboard. Just too far away.

Rowena came through from the scullery, lazily licking her teeth in a yawn. She seemed to sense the danger in the room, and scurried away again.

"Perhaps you'd care to explain this?" said Mrs. Cotton.

She brought her hands from behind her back, and I saw she wasn't holding a weapon of any sort. It was the Ouija cloth.

"It's mine," I said, reaching for it. She snatched it back, and with her other hand caught my wrist and pulled me close to her. "Devil child!" she hissed, and a spray of spittle landed on my face.

I tried to pull away, but she wouldn't let go. "Give it to me!" I shouted.

She twisted my arm back, and I cried out as pain blazed through my elbow and reached into my shoulder. "You bring this into my house!" she screamed.

"It's not your house!" I shouted back. "It will never be your house. Even if you kill everyone in it."

She pushed me to the floor and stood over me. "*What* did you say, child?"

"I know you killed them," I said. I crawled towards the sideboard, and she came behind me. "You killed them both, and I won't let you get away with it."

I put a hand on the sideboard and felt for the rolling pin. My fingertips found it, but it slipped away.

A whimper escaped my lips. "I won't let you—"

Her hands were on my shoulder and she yanked me up. I felt my dress tear, then I was dragged backwards through the kitchen. I couldn't find my footing on the stone floor. We were in the scullery now. One of her hands left me, and I heard the scraping of a door. Too late I realized what it was. The floor seemed to slip away and I landed with a thump in the cold space of the cellar, my ankle twisting painfully beneath me.

Mrs. Cotton stood with the trapdoor in her hand, looking down. Her chest rose and fell quickly. She disappeared, then came back with the Ouija cloth. She hurled it in my face. "You can stay down there with your devil's toy for now."

The door slammed shut.

Thirty-seven

CRADLING MY ANKLE IN THE PITCH DARKNESS, I felt gingerly along the bone. Nothing seemed out of place—it was just a nasty sprain. As the adrenaline died, so an ache set in through my other limbs. It was cold down in that cellar and I shivered in my cleaning smock. My head-scarf had come loose in the struggle and must have been lost up there in the kitchen.

How long would it be until Cook returned? A couple of hours? More? Had Mrs. Cotton planned to put me down here all along, or was it merely that her temper had got the better of her? I thought the latter. I expected her to come back at any minute with a weapon of some sort. What would she use? I wondered. A poker from the fire? A knife?

Fear took over again, forcing my breath out in ragged, uneven gasps. To die down here, bleeding in the darkness . . .

But the minutes passed and she didn't return. Gradually my breathing slowed, and I began to assess the situation with a clearer mind. If she did mean to finish me off before anyone returned, then she had picked a poor place to do it. She was strong, but would she be able to get my body out of this deep hole without help? And without leaving a trail of evidence?

At the hinge of the trapdoor was a pale crack of light, a narrow gap where the daylight could seep through. My eyes began to adjust to the gloom. There were weapons down here too—wine bottles in the stacks. I could strike her before she even made it to the bottom of the awkward steps.

The more I thought about it, the more I realized this was the safest place to be. All I had to do was sit tight and wait for someone else to arrive home. My shouts would alert them and then I would tell them everything. And that would be the end of Mrs. Cotton.

I tried to make myself comfortable against a pile of boxes, and had to shift one which was teetering. It was full of candles! I took one out and reached into my apron to find my matchbox, but it wasn't there. I must have left it beside His Lordship's fire. All I had was the wretched wooden fruit from the drawing room. I couldn't light a candle with that!

As I watched, a tiny glow appeared at the base of the wick. I thought my eyes were playing tricks, but the red ember grew, and suddenly the candle sparked into life, burning with a bright flame. I almost dropped it in shock.

The flame flickered—whether with my breath or something else, I didn't know.

"You're here," I whispered.

This time the flame didn't move. Melted wax began to drip over the side of the candle. I wedged it between two crates, staring at it in amazement. The cold cellar already felt warmer. Any lingering doubts were burnt away by that tiny flame.

But with the joy it brought came an immense frustration. She was here, beside me, around me, with me, but I couldn't see her. I couldn't hold her or speak to her . . .

Oh! But I *could*.

I had the Ouija. I had the ball.

My heart beat more quickly as I laid out the cloth on the floor. It was hard-packed earth and uneven, but that couldn't be helped. I placed the ball in the center and laid my fingers loosely on top.

"Mama?" I said. "Are you here?"

This time there was no pause. The ball rolled quickly to "Aye."

"Mama, don't worry," I said. "As soon as Sammy's

back, I'll tell him everything."

The ball rolled to "No." I hadn't even asked a question.

I brought it back to the center. I didn't understand.

"Why, Mama? They have to know. She killed His Lordship too. She killed my father—my real father."

The ball went again to "No." This couldn't be the uneven floor. It had happened in my room just the same.

I felt like shouting, but there was no one to shout at.

I forced my voice to remain calm, but I felt a little breathless.

"Why not tell me?" I said. "Is there something else? Someone else?"

The ball suddenly felt very warm. It traveled quickly to six different letters. By the time it reached the third, I knew the name it would spell.

When it stopped over the last letter, I picked it up and threw it across the room. It clattered between the wine bottles, then rolled slowly back towards my feet.

I couldn't believe it. I didn't want to.

The candle flickered and died.

The spirit was gone.

The name it had spelled was Samuel.

Thirty-eight

"NOT SAMMY!" I WHISPERED IN THE DARK.

I felt for the ball. Picked it up. I told myself that the spirit was confused.

Sammy loved his father, and my mother had shown him nothing but kindness. He was as gentle a creature as God made.

I asked the question again. "Was it Samuel, Mama?"

Now the ball didn't move.

"Mama, please!"

Nothing.

Footsteps creaked overhead, and I heard the bolt being drawn across. Mrs. Cotton was back.

I kicked the Ouija cloth into the recesses of the cellar as the trapdoor was lifted open. Light flooded in around a tall figure. It was Rob.

"Abi!" he said. His face was painted with concern.

"I thought I heard something. What are you doing down there?"

He held out an arm to me. I took his hand, and he heaved me up. "She locked me down here," I said.

"That woman!" he said. "What was it this time?"

"I don't know," I lied. "Where is she now?"

"Gone out to church, I think. I've just got back with Mr. Lock and the master."

"Samuel?"

"There's only one master now, isn't there?" said Rob.

Yes, I thought, I suppose there is.

I went about cleaning the family rooms in a daze. I wanted to be alone, but I was scared to be. Rob said that Samuel was resting upstairs, and I was glad of it. I'd been ready to lay my accusations in front of him, to brand Mrs. Cotton a murderer. What would I tell him now? The more I thought about it, the more I felt trapped.

I was polishing the mirror in the drawing room and asking questions of my own reflection, as if the answer lay within me. I had said to Mrs. Cotton's face what I thought, and I had feared she would take the ultimate revenge, but she hadn't. Instead she'd left me and gone off to church. What did that mean? Was that really the behavior of a killer?

More crucially, the Ouija had told me more than once that she was not the one. Such evidence—testimony from beyond the grave—would mean nothing before a judge, but I knew I couldn't deny it.

But Samuel? Dear Sammy. Why?

He claimed to have suspected that my mama and his father were in love, and he had always said he had next to no memory of his mother. In all but name, my mother had been his.

In the mirror, something caught my eye. When you've looked at a room as many times as I had, anything out of place tend to jump out. I recognized it as the photo Alexander had taken of Samuel and me, still hanging up to dry.

I left my polishing and walked over to it.

Upstairs, I heard Samuel's crutch and footstep creak across the room.

Carefully I unpinned the portrait. It was poorly exposed, and most of the room was cast in deep shadow. The candles and lamps we had brought into the library were reproduced as diffuse glowing blobs, like the street-lamps struggling to shine through the London smog.

I sat in the center, a faint smile on my face and hands crossed in my lap. Behind me stood Samuel, his hand on my shoulder and his chin lifted. In contrast to the rest of the room, our faces were quite clear and bright. It was the first time I'd ever seen my own likeness captured. I admit I was entranced.

Then I saw something else in the picture. A figure at the window.

I took a step backwards, colliding with the sofa and setting a vase rattling. Terror climbed across my chest. I wanted to look away, but my fingers still clutched the picture. My eyes were pulled to the left of the photograph.

I gasped.

It was little more than a shadow in the shape of a woman's torso, with a paler patch where her face might have been. It was just behind my right shoulder, and was turned not towards me, but Samuel. She had been there all along, watching.

"Something the matter?" said a voice.

I spun round to face Samuel and dropped the portrait.

"Sammy!" I said. "I'm so sorry. I was just cleaning. I was cleaning the mirror, and—"

"Slow down," he said, limping into the room on his crutch. "I know it's been a hard day. For all of us."

I couldn't let him see the photo. It would tell him

what I now felt sure of. But he saw it. "Oh," he said, "is that Alex's picture?" He sighed. "Let's take a look at it then."

I hesitated, but there was no way out of this. I stooped slowly and picked up the heavy paper. He took it with a smile. He made a show of holding it out at arm's length, and seemed to look for a good several seconds.

"Very handsome, eh?" He put it to one side on the cabinet, then began to hobble back towards the door.

He spoke over his shoulder. "What's for dinner later, do you know?"

"Cook's out for the moment," I said, thinking, *Your father died this morning, yet you're worried about your supper.*

When he was at the door, I looked back at the picture.

She stood there still, like an inky blot outside the window, with her pale face like the moon seen through mist.

Somehow, Samuel hadn't seen. I supposed that he never expected his accuser to rise again.

Thirty-nine

MRS. COTTON ATE EARLY, ON HER OWN IN THE sitting room. She made no mention of our fight, even when we passed each other at the top of the stairs. Normally she was so immaculately turned out, with not a stain or a speck of dust on her clothes, but now I noticed a smudge on her lace collar and strands of hair escaping from her bun.

For the first time since I'd known her, she looked vulnerable. I felt no guilt about what I'd said to her. It was too early for that.

But as the day wore on, thoughts tumbled over each other. Despite everything, I still couldn't fathom it: why —how—could he have done it?

Proof was the thing. I needed to be sure. Not ninety-nine parts in a hundred, but fully, without even the flicker of a doubt.

As Cook prepared dinner for Samuel and his ever-present guest Alexander Ambrose, I went back to the letter in my room and read it again. There was little about Sammy in the fragments that remained apart from that single line, "*You would be surprised how perceptive youngsters can be.*"

Was it possible, I wondered, that he had known of it since he was a boy? He told me he'd suspected something, but hadn't said how he felt about it. But surely a boy would be happy that his father had found love again, and especially if it was with the woman who had mothered him like her own?

And if he had been driven to murder, why wait until then, on the eve of his departure to war? Unless something had happened—something that tipped him over the edge. I read the fragments again, trying to decipher in those words anything that could explain it— to imagine my mother not as dear Mama, but as Susan Tamper, a woman in love. I didn't have any letters from Lord Greave—I didn't know if he'd ever even written any—but from the few words I could feel their different personalities.

> *Well, I am not, and I expressly <u>forbid</u> it. For a man of your—You scoff at appearances, but they are <u>everything</u>.*

The heavy underlining showed a tough woman— tougher than I remembered. Desperate, too, to make her point. He, on the other hand, seemed almost rash. He had wanted to tell people, that was clear. He had been ready to break with convention, and hang the consequences. It was my mother who had objected.

And then it hit me. Why hadn't I seen it before? If Lord Greave was to acknowledge my mother, he would have done so in only one way.

He had wanted to marry her!

Suddenly it made more sense. To admit to a mistress would have brought scorn, but to plan openly a marriage would at least be deemed acceptable, if irregular. A dent to propriety, but not to honor.

He'd planned to do so when she had first fallen pregnant, but she had refused to agree, worried how people would react, not least the inhabitants of Greave Hall. For her, it was only their child that had mattered— only me. So he had taken her in to live as a servant below stairs. How hard it must have been for them, together under the same roof yet so far apart!

The long deception—the years of living a lie—must have taken its toll. Had she finally come round to his way of thinking? Had she at last agreed to be the second Lady Greave? It made sense. Eleanor had been dead some twenty years.

But someone had prevented the couple fulfilling their dreams. Someone who stood to be disinherited by his father's mistress.

"Sammy," I whispered to myself.

I felt anger fizz along my veins. If only I had the other letters, I could be sure. Somehow he had found out his father's intentions and taken drastic steps. He'd poisoned her drink. I knew I couldn't prove it. There was no way I could bring Samuel before a judge and expect justice. But I wouldn't let him get away with it. Not again.

After dinner, when Mrs. Cotton had retired and Samuel had gone to the drawing room, he rang the bell. Knowing that Lock was relieving himself in the downstairs toilet, I went up.

I was surprised to find Sammy alone, sitting by the fire. There were two full glasses and a decanter of port beside him.

"Where's Alexander?" I said.

"I asked him to leave," he said sadly. "I wanted to be alone."

He sounded so convincing, and I watched him closely. What would Dr. Reinhardt, an expert on the signs of lying, have made of Samuel Greave?

"Do you miss him—your father, I mean?" I asked.

Sammy nodded. "It may be for the best, though, don't you think?"

For him, maybe.

He suddenly brightened, and gestured towards the decanter. "I thought you might like to join me for a drink, Abi."

A glass. Already poured. The room felt suddenly warmer, the fire banked in the hearth.

"I shouldn't," I said. "It's not right."

"Nonsense," he said. "You're family now."

While he reached for the glasses, I saw that his hand was bandaged around the palm.

A horrible image jumped into my head: his father clawing desperately as he struggled for life, trying to push his attacker off.

He selected the glass nearest to him, and handed it across. I looked at the ruby liquid. It seemed normal, but he would have mixed it carefully before I came into the room.

"Cheers," he said, raising his port.

I brought the glass to my lips, then lowered it again.

He sipped his slowly, watching me intently over the rim.

"Something wrong?" he asked.

I was glad of the dim lighting, as I could feel my face flushing. I imagined it was as red as the drink he had offered me.

"Erm . . . no," I managed, sniffing the liquid and smiling. "I'm just not sure I'll like the taste."

"Only one way to find out though," he said. "Mr. Lock told me this was one of the best in the cellar."

I didn't know what to do. The hairs stood up on the back of my neck.

"What happened to your hand?" I said.

He looked at it quickly. "Oh," he said. "It was that blasted cat."

"Rowena?" I said.

"Is that her name? Yes. Vicious little thing, isn't she?"

No, I thought. She isn't.

Rowena had never scratched anybody as long as I knew her. Samuel's father had fought back, but didn't have the strength. My mother hadn't even had the chance.

Was it rat poison, I wondered, or something more deadly? Would it act slowly, burning through my insides while I slept? Or did Samuel plan for me to die now, right in front of him, slumping over in my chair after half a glass?

I put the glass down. "I'm not thirsty."

He breathed a long sigh through his nose and leaned forward, gripping the armrest of his chair.

"You know," he said coldly, "it's rude to refuse someone's hospitality."

The door was only a few paces away. I knew I could reach it long before him, but something made me stay seated. I had to be sure. Not ninety-nine parts in a hundred, but fully.

"Sammy?" I said.

Half his face was in shadow, and one eye gleamed like an ember in the reflected light of the fire. He had always been a man of two sides. "Yes, Abi?"

I thought through my words carefully and spoke slowly, looking him in that one blazing eye.

"What would you do, Sammy, if you knew someone had done a terrible thing, but that they wouldn't be punished for it?"

He cocked his head a little. "What a strange thing to say."

I smiled. "I suppose it is. But what would you do?"

His eyes looked behind me to the door. I felt a tiny prickle of fear.

"My aunt would say that God sees everything," he said, more quietly now. "Is this about her?"

"No," I said. "This isn't about her." He swallowed uncomfortably. "Do you think that though, Sammy? Do you think God sees everything we do wrong?"

"I say," he said, "this is a damned strange conversation." He took a longer gulp from his glass.

"I don't think that God sees everything," I said. "I think sometimes it's up to us. You know—to make people pay for what they do wrong."

"Then I would advise you," he said, placing his glass down beside the untouched one, "to be very careful."

In that moment, I was sure.

"Goodnight, Samuel," I said, quickly standing up and slipping away to the door. I couldn't bear to look at him any longer.

"Sleep well, sister," he said to my departing back.

I hardly slept at all that night. Every time I drifted off, I thought I heard a noise on the stairs, and sat up in bed panting until I was sure it was just my imagination. Samuel had managed to get up His Lordship's stairs.

Why not mine?

Eventually I took my blankets and pillows and went down the short corridor into Lizzy's old room. There, at least, I managed an hour's sleep before morning.

The cards of condolence began to arrive with the first post. Soon there were upwards of a dozen piled on the stand beside the front door.

Samuel made a show of reading them, but I caught his look at odd moments and saw that he was smiling. Actually *smiling*.

"Father had a lot of friends," he said.

I felt sick. How had I never seen what a monster he was? Now he had the power. And he knew it.

I was polishing the dining room table, when I heard the sound of hooves outside, and the coachman calling his horses to a stop. A hackney carriage pulled up in front of the window. Mr. Carter climbed out with another man of similar age. The solicitor and his companion were both dressed in black, as suited the family in mourning. Mr. Carter carried a leather satchel.

I stopped what I was doing and went to open the door, just as Lock came up the stairs and Samuel struggled on his crutch from the sitting room.

"You didn't have to come in person," said Samuel, gesturing to the cards.

"I'm afraid I did," said Mr. Carter. "This is my colleague Mr. Lassiter. Do you have somewhere we can speak in private?"

A look of confusion passed over Samuel's face, but he smothered it with a smile. "Of course," he said. "Come to the library. Abi, take the gentlemen's coats, will you?"

As I did so, Mr. Carter turned to me. "Are you Miss Abigail Tamper?" he said.

I wasn't used to being addressed by my name by strangers. "Yes, sir," I replied.

"Well, you should join us," he said. "Mr. Lock too, if you don't mind."

"I thought you said it was a private meeting," said Samuel curtly.

Mr. Carter looked at Samuel with tired eyes. "They need to be there," he said simply.

Samuel's face tightened and flushed, but I was worried too. What possible use could I be to these gentlemen?

"Very well," he said.

I stayed at the back of the group while we trooped into the library, then closed the door. Carter sat down on the little settee and opened his satchel. He laid out a sheaf of papers on a low table in front of him and placed two envelopes beside it.

"Listen, what's this all about?" snapped Samuel.

Mr. Carter didn't react to his rudeness. "As you know," he said calmly, "Carter & Carter is responsible for executing your late father's estate—"

"Yes, I know," interrupted Samuel. "I have a copy of the will here somewhere." He gestured towards the desk. "My friend Alex has had a good look over it for me, and there's nothing—"

"If you'd let me finish," said Mr. Carter, holding up his hand. "Just over a year ago, His Lordship came to our offices and asked to make several . . . amendments to his Last Will and Testament."

"Amendments?" said Samuel.

"In effect," put in Mr. Lassiter, "he made a single substantial change."

Samuel raised his fist to his mouth as if to stop himself from speaking. His face had gone from red to bloodless white, and his one good leg was shaking.

"Master Greave, your father has left his entire estate"—Here Mr. Carter paused and looked at me—"to Miss Tamper."

Forty

I STOOD BACK AGAINST THE WALL, FOR FEAR I
would otherwise collapse on to the carpet. I wasn't
sure if I'd heard correctly. "Did you say, to me?" I asked.

"That's right, miss," said Mr. Lassiter, bobbing his
head.

Samuel didn't speak for what seemed like minutes,
but it could only have been a few seconds. He stared
at me as if seeing me for the first time. Then his gaze
traveled to Mr. Carter and his colleague. Mr. Lock, I
noticed, hadn't batted an eyelid.

"The will must be wrong," said Samuel.

"I assure you," said Mr. Carter, "Lord Greave was
quite specific."

Samuel waved a hand dismissively. "He wasn't in
a fit state to be specific, gentlemen. His mind was not
functioning properly. Surely that invalidates the will?"

"Sir, you yourself said not two days ago that his mental infirmity was only a recent development. You'll see from the date on the will that this was signed on January fourth last year."

Three days after my mother died.

He'd left everything to me. To his daughter.

Samuel snorted.

"Master Greave," said Mr. Carter patiently, "your father's wishes are clear, and they are countersigned by two witnesses."

"What witnesses?" said Samuel.

"Mr. Lassiter here," said Mr. Carter, "and Trevor Lock."

Samuel turned to stare at Mr. Lock, his eyebrows lifted in incredulity.

Lock straightened his back. "I obeyed His Lordship, sir."

"But she's just a scullery maid," said Samuel, gesturing to me. I fancy only I caught the curl of his lip which accompanied the words.

"I expect she will find her own scullery maid now," said Mr. Lassiter.

"We'll see about that!" said Samuel, shaking his head. "It's most irregular. I shall have to—"

"Sir," interrupted Mr. Carter. He picked up one of

the envelopes and offered it to Samuel. "His Lordship wrote this letter to be given to you upon his death."

Samuel snatched at the envelope, and tore it open. His eyes scanned the lines quickly. Whatever it said, his face betrayed no emotion other than a slight twitching at the corner of his lips.

"Did any of you read it?" he asked.

"Of course not, sir," said Mr. Carter. "We value our clients' privacy above all else."

"And you?" Samuel questioned Mr. Lock.

The butler shook his head.

"Very good," he said. He tucked the letter into his pocket and, twisting his body awkwardly, strutted out of the room on his crutch.

Together we listened to him climb the stairs. When his door closed, I saw the attention of the three men was upon me.

"And this is for you," said Mr. Carter, holding out the second envelope. "Mr. Lock, I think that concludes our business here."

The butler nodded and went to fetch the coats. Mr. Carter turned to me and smiled.

"Well, my dear, I will not presume to understand the whims of my clients, but I will always respect them. This place is yours now, and no doubt you will need guidance in understanding and governing.We at Carter & Carter are here to help. Mr. Lassiter will visit again tomorrow, if that suits you."

Suits me? "No one's ever asked that before!" I said.

Both lawyers smiled. "Well, you must get used to it, Miss Tamper."

And then he shook my hand! A gentleman! I was so gobsmacked I dropped into a curtsy. That made them laugh again.

Mr. Lock showed them to the door, and I sat down at the desk—my desk!—to read the letter. I hadn't even thought what I would do next, but I knew that the minutes, hours, and days to come would throw everything into chaos. I simply couldn't fathom what had happened.

I opened the envelope slowly with the letter knife. I pulled out the single sheet of paper as Mrs. Cotton's quick footsteps arrived at the library door.

"What on earth do you think you're doing sitting there, Miss Tamper? Get up at once!"

I stood up. Old habits are hard to shake. I wanted to shout at her that I'd had enough, that she couldn't hurt me any more, but I couldn't. It was too unreal.

"I–"

Mr. Lock appeared at her elbow. "Mrs. Cotton, if I could have a word."

"Can't it wait?"

"No, ma'am, it cannot," he said.

There was a steel in his voice that I think neither of us had heard before. The housekeeper followed him out towards the hall. I stood just out of sight, listening, clutching the door frame.

I couldn't hear what the butler said, so hushed were his tones, but Mrs. Cotton spoke very clearly. "Is this some sort of joke?"

"No, Lillian, it isn't. We answer to Miss Tamper now."

I stepped out into the hall myself, and Mrs. Cotton gave me a look of pure terror, as if my very presence could hurt her. She backed away towards the stairs, flailing with her hand for the banister. "Where's Samuel?" she said.

"I believe he went upstairs," said Mr. Lock.

Her foot found the stairs, and she hurried up, shouting, "Samuel? Samuel!" like a drowning woman crying for rescue.

Forty-one

MR. LOCK OFFERED TO TELL ROB AND COOK, and I told him I would much appreciate that. I didn't know if I had the strength to do it myself. Instead, I sat down again at the desk and read the letter from Lord Greave. It was only half a page.

> *Dearest Abigail,*
>
> *I thought I understood what courage was. I thought I had seen it on the decks of the ships at Navarino, when men met their deaths with shouts of defiance. I fancied myself courageous to stand alongside them and call on death too. If you are reading this letter, then death has heard my call.*
>
> *But courage is being able to speak the truth, no matter what the censure or what the sacrifice. I am a coward. I knew a terrible truth, but I said nothing. I hope you can forgive me.*
>
> *Your loving father,*
> *Nathaniel Greave*

At first, I felt only anger. Anger that he had never acknowledged me as his daughter or my mother as his love. Anger that he had never faced Samuel for what he had done. For what else could the "terrible truth" be? My father had carried with him a burden that had driven him to madness—the knowledge of his son's inhuman deed. What a price to pay for his cowardice!

And now, I realized, that truth would remain hidden forever. This house might be mine, but what did that mean if he got away with his awful crimes? I'd have given it all back on the spot if it could change anything.

Samuel would have to leave, of course. I couldn't imagine him wanting to stay, not after all that had happened. Perhaps the War Office would find him a job. Perhaps Alexander would take pity on his friend. In that moment, he could have starved on the streets for all I cared. Even to look at him again would have made my rage boil.

Shortly after, I folded up the letter and put it into the desk drawer. Then I went downstairs. Cook and Rob were deep in conversation at the table, and both stood up when I came in.

"You don't have to do that!" I said.

"I suppose I can call you m'lady for real now, then?" said Rob.

"That you can, Mr. Willmett," I replied.

His face broke into a gap-toothed smile, and I laughed too.

"Well, what now, miss?" said Cook. "Would you like me to get you some dinner?"

"I'd like you to take the rest of the day off," I said. I needed to straighten out my thoughts, and I could fend for myself.

"Well, thank you, miss," said Cook.

"You too," I said to Rob. "Do you know where Mr. Lock is?" I added.

Rob said he'd gone back to his room, so I bade them goodbye and left. On my way out, Rowena brushed against my leg. She was the only one not fazed by all this.

I knocked on Mr. Lock's door.

"Come in," said a weak voice.

I pushed open the door and saw him sitting in his chair. I'd never been in this room before—an hour before, it would have been unthinkable—and it was smaller than I'd expected. There was a bed, a wardrobe, and a table with a single chair. No window. The floor was stone, and covered with two threadbare rugs. The fire, I was surprised to see, was unlit.

"What can I do for you, Miss Tamper?" he said. He looked anxious, unsure of himself.

I took a seat. "You can tell me the truth," I said.

The wrinkles around his eyes lifted a little. "The truth?"

I nodded. "Did you always know about my mother and His Lordship?"

"It is not my place to speculate," he said quickly.

I remembered Samuel's words. "Well, things are going to change around here," I replied. "You can speculate all you want from now on."

He laughed at that, and his face shed its years again. Perhaps he had been handsome once, just like my mother said.

"That will take some getting used to," he said.

"Let's start now, then," I said. "I've seen the letter you tried to burn." He lifted his bushy eyebrows in surprise. "His Lordship was my father," I added. "You knew that all along."

Mr. Lock looked down at his feet, then up again. "I suppose I knew," he said. "I'm not as sharp-eyed as Lillian, but I'm not simple either. I could see it when they were together. Just little things—shared glances, something in the air when they brushed past each other . . ."

"They loved each other," I said, my tears welling up.

"They must have done," said Mr. Lock. "He left you all this, didn't he?'

I wanted him to say more, but it was like getting blood out of a stone.

"And Mrs. Cotton knew? About the letter too?"

"It seems like it," he said. "Though I don't see how. She told me where it was, and that I had to burn it straight away. She said it was for the best. I don't—I don't know why I did it."

He couldn't look me in the eye anymore.

"What happened up there?" I asked. "I saw you running down the stairs."

"I had a funny turn, that's all."

"It was more than that," I said.

"Please," he said, "I don't want to say."

He was pale again, and wringing his hands. Just an old man, afraid. I didn't press him further.

"Well," he said, pulling himself together, "you can't be sleeping up in the attic any more. Shall I prepare Her Ladyship's old room for you?"

"No," I said. "I'm fine where I am for now. I've told the other two to take the day off. Why don't you too?"

"Very well, miss. And what will you do?"

I hadn't thought much about that, but I made a decision on the spur of the moment.

"I think I'll go for a walk," I said. "In the Park."

"Then you'll be needing keys," he said.

"Yes," I smiled. "I suppose I will."

Mr. Lock gave me his, and I went upstairs to get changed into my blue dress. I found a plain shawl in Lizzy's room and took it with me. I was sure she wouldn't mind. First thing next day, I planned to go to her sister's place and find her. I couldn't begin to imagine what she'd say.

I took the servants' stairs out of habit, but left by the front door. Across the road, I entered the Park and walked slowly around the perimeter, marveling at the great barracks building, and then at Buckingham Palace. What must the Queen feel like when she was in there? Surely not at home. It was too big for anyone, just like Greave Hall.

When I was opposite the house, on the other side of the lake, I looked back. It really was a very grand residence—one of the finest on the edge of the Park.

There was so much to do, and I felt more alone than ever. Cook and Mr. Lock could help with day-to-day matters, but I knew nothing of property or money, nothing of business affairs, or hiring staff.

A high-pitched voice called out, "Is that you, Abigail?"

A cart had pulled up on the road nearest to me, some thirty yards away. It was Adam. I hadn't seen him since I had snapped at him a few days ago, but his face was a welcome sight now. I ran across the grass to the road.

"What you doing out?" he said. "That housekeeper been at the drink?"

After everything that had happened, he was so normal.

"Something like that," I said. "Listen, Adam, I'm sorry about before."

He waved his hand. "Think nothing of it," he said. "I gave up tryin' to understand women long ago."

"Oh, yes?" I laughed. "You've known a lot of women, have you?"

"'Ave I?" he said, with mock surprise. "I'll tell you sometime, but it's a long story."

"You can tell me next time you come around."

"Right you are, miss," he said. "See you tomorrow, then."

He trundled off.

I've got quite a long story for you too, I thought.

When I got back, Lock told me that Samuel had taken a cab to his club in town, and that Mrs. Cotton had not come out of her room as far as he knew. The light was fading, so I made myself a sandwich and took it upstairs to Lizzy's room. I ate it, then lay back on the bed.

Perhaps I could manage all this after all.

I didn't mean to fall asleep, but I must have been more tired than I thought. I woke thinking that I'd heard a creak on the stairs, and sat up in a daze. It was pitch black outside. What time was it?

Another creak. This time I was sure.

I swung my legs off the bed, and listened. I could hear breathing too. Labored, heavy breathing.

Someone was climbing the attic stairs.

I knew who it was at once. These were not the regular steps of Mrs. Cotton. It was not Lizzy or Rob. This was an uneven gait. I heard the soft knocking of a crutch. Samuel.

I'd thought he would surely sleep at his club, so if he was back here, there was only one reason for his visit.

I should have slept downstairs.

The steps reached the top of the stairs. Why hadn't I listened to Mr. Lock? I looked around the room for something to defend myself with, and the steps began to move away.

Of course—he was going to my room. But I was in here. I had a chance.

I tiptoed to the wardrobe and pulled open the door as quietly as possible. There was nothing inside. The clothes rail was empty.

He would have seen I wasn't in bed by now.

The clothes rail was a wooden pole, three feet long, suspended on two brackets but not screwed in. I unhooked it and pulled it out of the wardrobe, but on the way it bumped against the door. The sound was deafening.

Suddenly, outside the door, the footsteps approached more quickly.

Knock-step, knock-step, knock-step.

Then Samuel was standing in the doorway.

"Hello, little sister," he said.

Forty-two

Sammy's hair was plastered to his forehead, and his face was dark. I could smell alcohol on his breath.

"What do you want?" I said.

"I want what you've stolen from me," he replied.

I held the pole in front of me like a sword. "I've not stolen anything."

He coughed, a hacking choking cough, with his mouth pressed into the crook of his elbow. "You've stolen everything that belongs to me!"

The clothes rail seemed pathetic now. The end was trembling. "Well, I won't give you anything," I said.

Samuel shook his head. "I thought you might say that," he went on, "which is why I've brought this." Reaching inside his jacket, he took out a paring knife from the kitchen. The words dried up in my throat.

"Would anyone really be surprised," he continued,

"if you decided to take your own life, Abi? Up here, all alone. No mother, no father, no friends. You've had a tough year, haven't you?"

I couldn't tear my eyes from the wicked blade, catching the glint of silver moonlight from outside.

"Let me out!" I said, louder this time. Mrs. Cotton must have been able to hear me.

Samuel laughed. He had read my thoughts. "My aunt isn't down there," he said. "You'll have to scream louder than that if anyone's going to hear you. But you know how thick these walls are. It's your house, after all."

I screamed as loudly as I could. If someone were outside in the lane, they'd hear me even if Rob couldn't from the china closet where he slept.

"Try again," he sneered. I screamed once more, until I thought my throat would tear. "Help me! Someone help me!"

I realized with horror that if Rob had gone out and wasn't back yet, that left only Mr. Lock and Cook, and they were in the basement—she's dead drunk, no doubt, and he without a window for the sound to reach in.

Samuel spoke again from the doorway. "You think you're so clever, don't you, Miss Tamper? You think you deserve all this."

"More than you," I hissed. "You killed two innocent people."

"Innocent?" he said, suddenly flaring up and moving towards me. "Innocent? The gentleman who couldn't keep his hands off the nurse!"

"They were in love!" I shouted.

I swung the pole and cracked him across the head. He dropped the knife and gripped his face with a muffled shout. I hit him again, and he fell backwards into the corridor. His crutch fell beside him. I rushed past, but he must have gripped my ankle, because I fell face down at the top of the stairs. The air was knocked out of me and I couldn't breathe.

His weight pressed against my back as he heaved himself up on to my body. I managed to roll over, but his hands found my neck.

"None of you are innocent," he said. Spit flecked from his mouth, dripping on to my face. There was blood too, from a cut above his eye. His fingers tightened on my throat, but even with both hands I couldn't push him off.

I felt the blood pumping through my temples and behind my eyes. In the shadows I could see his face, contorted with fury. His teeth were bared, and the veins stood up across his forehead. I writhed and kicked, but he was too strong.

Was it really going to end here, with my back on the floorboards, choked to death in the attic?

My vision started to blur, and my eyes felt as if they would explode. I tried to kick at Samuel's stump, but my legs had no strength left in them. My hands were still tugging at his fingers as the world started to blacken at the edges.

I felt something—it was the bandage on his hand. I tore it off and felt for the scabbed skin underneath. With my last remaining strength, I dug my nails into his flesh.

Samuel howled and pulled back, releasing my throat.

Air rushed into my lungs. I squirmed, lifting my knee, then brought my foot down on the stump of his amputated leg. He screamed and rolled sideways, taking all his weight off me.

I saw his crutch and reached for it as I scrambled to my feet. Just as he managed to raise himself up on to his foot at the top of the narrow stairs, I rammed it hard into his chest.

His arms wheeled as he tried to regain his balance. His hand went to the wall to steady himself. I shoved again, grunting as I did so.

Samuel toppled backwards, his short leg jutting upwards. I flinched as his head cracked into the first step, but he didn't stop there. Without a cry, he fell down the narrow stairs, rolling over and over like a rag doll. The stairs shook as he crashed to the bottom.

Breathing heavily, I stared at his crumpled form. My first thought was that he was dead, but he moaned softly and pushed himself upright.

Gripping the crutch, I descended the stairs, half-stumbling. He disappeared out of sight, shuffling across the floor on his backside. When I reached him he had his back against Mrs. Cotton's bedroom door. I raised the crutch, anger surging through my arms. I wanted to bash his brains out.

"Do it!" he gasped. "Do it, and you'll never even know the truth."

"What truth?" I shouted, fighting the urge to bring the end of the crutch down on his sweating face. "That you're a killer?"

"That it was an accident," he said, his chest rising and falling.

"You poisoned her," I said, tears running down my cheeks. "Just like you tried to poison me."

Samuel shook his head violently. "He told me he was going to marry her." His eyes were ablaze once more. "He told me he was in love, that he felt alone." His face twisted into a sneer. "I couldn't let him shame our family. Think what they would have said! Marrying one of the staff—a nurse, for pity's sake!"

"So you killed her?" I said.

He shook his head again. "He was so miserable, so wretched. I wanted to put the old fool out of his misery. I took up his brandy, like I always did." He laughed bitterly. "Ever the dutiful son. She must have sneaked up there somehow. Must've drunk it instead. I never meant it to happen like that. If she could just have stayed put . . ." His words trailed off into bitter laughter.

If he was lying, he was a fine actor. His eyes were shot through with blood and sweat covered his face, mingling with the mucus running from his nose. I saw it at once. Samuel leaving the brandy tray, my mother entering through their secret way, Nathaniel Greave offering her a drink . . .

"You're still a murderer," I said.

"And there's nothing you can do," he replied. "If you bash my brains out against this door, you will be a murderer too. Think of it, *sister!* The scullery maid who murdered the war hero! They'll have you dangling from a rope before the week is out!"

My determination wavered as a feeling of helplessness overcame me. My arms felt suddenly exhausted and I let the crutch fall at my side. Samuel was right.

"I'll tell everyone," I said. "I'll make sure you never set foot in this house again."

"And who will believe you?" he said. "Without another witness it's your word against mine. I'm sure my aunt will vouch for me."

"Aye, but we won't," said an Irish voice.

I turned to see Cook, Mr. Lock, and Rob standing at the top of the main stairs. She was carrying a cleaver from the kitchen and the butler a poker. Rob was dressed only in his nightshirt.

The smile disappeared from Samuel's face. "Get off those stairs!" he said.

None of them moved. "I think we'll be summoning the constables," said Miss McMahon. She held out a hand. "You should come with us, Abigail."

The following hours passed in a confusion of visitors and growing weariness. Rob stood guard over Samuel until the police arrived. Cook wrapped me in a blanket beside the newly lit fire in the kitchen, and made me a cup of Mrs. Cotton's favorite hot chocolate. Repeated knocking on the housekeeper's door brought no response. Looking in, Mr. Lock found it to be empty. He told us her clothes and jewelry were missing too.

Constable Armstrong spent a long time with the butler in his parlor, while his colleagues took Samuel aside to the drawing room. There were conventions to be kept, even then, with master and servant in their rightful place. From the kitchen, we could hear Sammy ranting and raving about the injustices he had suffered.

The policemen took down statements from all three of the staff about what they had overheard. I answered the constable's probing questions about what I had found out and when. I was worried that I wouldn't be believed, but I later learned that our stories concurred to such a degree, there was little doubt we were all telling the truth. Before dawn Dr. Ingle arrived to examine the bruising on my neck and found that it was consistent with having been throttled. As he left the house he patted me on the shoulder, and said that I was the most unfortunate patient of his but, from what he had heard, also the luckiest.

The constables suggested that Samuel might like to recover his sobriety at the police station house in Pimlico. He was sobbing as he was taken away. I wondered if I'd ever see him again. Gradually the house emptied, leaving just the four of us—four servants without a master. I was tired, but there would be no sleep, I was sure. I drifted instead into the sitting room, where Lock had insisted on lighting the fire. I opened the curtains myself, and looked out as the sun came up in the east.

The grass was covered with a thick frost, and the street outside was silent. I noticed the first of the snowdrops were lifting their heads, defiant in the face of the cold.

"What date is it?" I asked Mr. Lock.

He stood stiffly from the fire, as the kindling crackled beneath the coals.

"The seventeenth of February, Miss," he said.

My birthday.

ABIGAIL MERCHANT OBE
(17TH FEBRUARY, 1840–22ND APRIL, 1933)

By the time of her death at the age of ninety-three, Mrs. Merchant's name was synonymous with the charity that occupied her adult life. She will be fondly remembered by all who knew her as a warm-hearted and generous woman whose rise to wealthy philanthropist never distanced her from her humble roots. Indeed, friends still recall her remark when dining with the Queen at a Buckingham Palace charity dinner: she dropped her soup spoon on the carpet, and before the butler could replace it, Abigail had plucked it up herself and proceeded to eat her first course. "When you've had to polish as many of these as I have," she said, "it rather changes your perspective."

Abigail Merchant was born Abigail Tamper in relative obscurity in the West London suburb of Acton in 1840. Her father, James Tamper, was a petty thief, who was caught, tried and transported to Australia in her early years, though exact records were lost in a fire in 1852. Her mother, Susan Tamper, in order to provide for her only child, took a role in service at the house of Nathaniel Greave, a naval lord and landowner. Fellow inhabitants recall her being a diligent and respectful addition to the household staff, who managed her working life and the care of a small child with great professionalism.

Tragedy dogged Abigail's early years, and in many ways her story is typical of those times. Her mother perished in 1854, during the cholera epidemic that swept through London. The esteem and affection in which Susan Tamper was held is evident in the manner of Abigail's upbringing. She was taught to read, and play the piano with some proficiency, although she would later modestly claim that she could barely manage a note.

It has been suggested that the young Abigail Tamper's altruism may have been born in her early years, when the son of Lord Greave, Samuel, with whom Abigail was known to share a close bond, returned injured from the war on the Crimean Peninsula in early 1855. Abigail was instrumental in nursing him back to health. Scandal was to later envelop the family, with Samuel accused of foul play in the death of his own father. The accusations were never heard in court, as Samuel took his own life while in custody.

This was to be a watershed in young Abigail's life. In Lord Greave's Last Will and Testament, which is in the possession of the Greave Foundation to this day, Abigail was named sole heir to the Greave estates. She later spoke of her shock at this sudden reversal of fortune. At the time, there was some rumour that the elderly Lord Greave was in fact Abigail's father, though this has never been substantiated. Rather it is thought his remarkable act of generosity was owing to Abigail's care for Lord Greave's wounded son.

Certainly Miss Tamper put this new-found wealth to good use, taking in and caring for the widows and children of deceased servicemen. She was assisted in these early efforts by former members of the household staff, including her lifelong friend Elizabeth Henshall.

Throughout the latter half of the last century, the Greave Foundation expanded its portfolio of properties through charitable donations, and is reckoned conservatively to have helped over two thousand of this country's most vulnerable women and children. Mrs. Merchant remained at the helm until ill-health began to take its toll last year, and she died peacefully in her bed on Tuesday. Her husband Adam, a former coal delivery boy, passed on in the spring of 1919. She is survived by their daughter, Rowena, three grandchildren, and four great grandchildren.

She will be buried, as she wished, beside her mother in the graveyard of St. Martin's-in-the-Fields this Saturday, and her departure from this world is certain to be well attended. Condolences should be sent to The Greave Foundation, 112 Park Avenue, London.